THE
THIRD
EYE

THE THIRD EYE

MOLLIE HUNTER

HARPER & ROW, **Publishers**
New York · Hagerstown · San Francisco · London

Library of Congress Cataloging in Publication Data
McIlwraith, Maureen Mollie Hunter McVeigh, date
    The third eye.

    SUMMARY: Jinty's intuitive sense, her third eye,
brings her close to the old Earl as he struggles
with the Ballinford doom.
    [1. Scotland—Fiction] I. Title.
PZ7.M18543Tg   [Fic]   78-22159
ISBN 0-06-022676-5
ISBN 0-06-022677-3 lib. bdg.

Michael,
    It was a long haul, but
    "We climbed the hill thegither."
    With my love and thanks
    for all your helping hands,
                                M.H.

THE
THIRD
EYE

I

On the day that Jinty was due to be questioned, she left the house with her mother at ten o'clock in the morning. Outside the door, her mother gave her the long buff envelope that was stamped in large black capitals with the words, ON HIS MAJESTY'S SERVICE.

"You'd better take that now," she said, "seeing it's addressed to you. You might need to have it when you're called into the Procurator Fiscal's office."

She locked the door, put the key in its usual hiding place, and they crossed the street to wait for the ten past ten bus to Haimston. From the bus stop then, they could see that the door of Archie Meikle's smithy was open and that his son, Tom, was working at the forge; but there was no sign of Archie himself coming out to wait for the bus, and Jinty wondered if he had been told to report to the Fiscal at a different time from the one in her own letter. Her mother seemed to be thinking on the same lines. As the bus hove in sight she gave a last glance at the smithy and said,

"Meikle must have got the ten past nine bus."

Jinty nodded, and then voiced the idea in her own mind. "Or he might have got a lift in with Lord Garvald."

"Pigs might fly," her mother retorted. "It was all very well for Meikle to have been thick as thieves with the old Earl, but Garvald's very different from the man his father was."

As they took their seats in the bus she added, "And remember, it's Lord Garvald who's the Earl of Ballinford now. That's what the Procurator will call him, too—or maybe he'll say 'the present Earl,' and talk about the father as 'the late Earl.' But anyway, just watch you don't get mixed up between the two of them when you're answering the questions."

The bus drew away past the smithy and the school, past the single row of whitewashed cottages facing the fields of Ballinford Mains Farm on the opposite side of the street.

"The snowdrops are out," her mother said, glancing at the small gardens in front of the houses, but that was something that Jinty didn't want to see. Snowdrops belonged to an old memory, a painful one she had locked away three years before that time. She kept her gaze ahead, watching the church spire appearing at the other side of the rise beyond the Post Office. Mr. Elphinston, the minister, was pinning a notice on the board at the gate of the churchyard. She saw the small, thin figure stretching up to control the paper flapping in the wind, and then the bus was out of the village and swinging around at the crossroads to take the fork that pointed to the market town of Haimston.

"Two to the Sheriff Court Building," her mother told the conductor. She spoke in a low voice, glancing around to make sure no one else on the bus was listening; and when the conductor repeated loudly, "Two to the Sheriff Court," she frowned annoyance at him. Jinty wondered why she bothered. There was nobody in the village, after all, who didn't know about the three of them—herself and Archie Meikle and Lord Garvald—being called to the Procurator Fiscal's office; and the word of that was bound to be spread elsewhere, eventually. She fingered the buff envelope on her lap, and surreptitiously began to edge her own summons out of it. The date appeared—14th February, 1935; and opposite that, her own name and address in full—Janet Beatrice Morrison, Rose Cottage, Ballinford, West Lothian, Scotland.

"You'll have that dog-eared," her mother said sharply. "Stop fiddling with it."

"I was wondering—" Jinty said. "Mam, what exactly does the Procurator Fiscal do? Why does it have to be him that hears my—my evidence?"

"He's the chief law officer of the county—for criminal cases, that is," her mother said; "and so it's his job to inquire into any fatal accident or sudden death."

3

Jinty sat listening to the wheels of the bus swishing out *"accident, accident, accident . . ."* If she had to swear on oath—!

"Mam," she said presently, "when you give evidence, what sort of an oath do you have to swear?"

"It's—er—it's—Now let me see." Her mother considered in silence for a few moments and then said slowly, "I swear by Almighty God, as I shall answer to Him at the Great Day of Judgment, that the evidence I shall give, shall be the truth, the whole—"

"But they couldn't!" Jinty interrupted. Alarm made her speak louder than she had intended, and realizing her mother's disapproval at this, she dropped her voice to an urgent whisper. "They couldn't make *me* take an oath like that! I'm a minor. I'm only fourteen."

"That's old enough to understand the words of the oath," her mother retorted. "And if the Sheriff thinks so too, being a minor doesn't enter into it. But anyway—"

Looking puzzled now, she turned in her seat to study Jinty's face. "What's got into you, all of a sudden? You're not going to give your evidence in court—not yet, at least. I told you so. I told you this was to be a private examination."

Jinty answered silently, *"But you didn't tell me I wouldn't have to take an oath before I answered the questions. And I'll have more of a chance against the Fiscal, won't I, if I don't have to tell the whole truth?"* Aloud, she began on a halting reply that she hoped would conceal the true cause of her alarm over the oath; then was relieved to see her mother nod and glance away, as if losing interest in the conversation. She looked ahead through the windscreen of the bus, and saw another bus coming towards them.

"There's the bus from Haimston," she said, and her mother gave a further nod that acknowledged this.

The road was narrow. The driver of their own bus pulled it close to the verge on his side, the other driver did the same for his. The pace of both slowed to a careful crawl, and as the bus from Haimston passed by their own, Jinty had a quick, head-and-shoulders view of a young woman with golden-red hair sitting on the far side of it.

"It's Meg!" she exclaimed. "Mam, that's Meg on the other bus."

Her mother didn't answer right away. It was only after the Haimston bus had passed that she said, "I expect it is. She wrote to say she meant to visit me today."

"But—" Jinty had been craning to look after the Haimston bus, and the word brought her jerking around to her mother again. "But you knew we'd be out today. And you locked the door!"

"That's right." The face that met her own look of dismayed protest had the same unyielding expression it had worn on the night Meg had left home. "Meg's no daughter of mine now."

"*But she knows where the key is kept,*" Jinty told herself; and sat back in her seat thinking of Meg arriving at the locked door. What would she do then? Look for the key? Take the next bus from the village back to

Haimston? Staring out at the bare fields trundling past them, and suddenly aching with the longing to feel again the warm ebullience of her sister's presence, she willed Meg to look for the key, to unlock the door, to go in and wait for their homecoming. . . .

The spire of Haimston Parish Church came in sight, and then the tall square tower of the Corn Exchange. The bus entered Academy Street. It was 10:45, time for the break in morning school. As the bus passed by the group of buildings that dominated the rest of the street, Jinty glimpsed a cluster of the pupils who had been her classmates since she had gone up, two years previously, from the village school to Haimston Academy; and under her breath she muttered, *"Vivat Academia!"*

"What did you say?" her mother asked, and lamely she answered,

"It was just a joke." Just a school joke, a greeting they were all in the habit of giving one another as a sort of jibe at themselves and the way they all had to knuckle under to the intellectual pretensions of the Academy. But how could she explain that sort of thing to her mother when she knew perfectly well the kind of answer she would get?

"It wasn't any kind of a joke for me to make the sacrifices it needed to send you and your sisters to the Academy."

"Well? Are you going to keep it all to yourself?" Her mother was looking at her, waiting for her to go on.

She shook her head, and then began trying to ex-

6

plain after all, so that her mother would keep looking at her instead of being even further upset by having to see that they were now passing the corner where Dave Ferguson had his garage, and that Dave himself was standing beside one of the cars at its door.

When the bus reached the main square of Haimston, the two of them got out of it and crossed towards the Sheriff Court Building. There was a flight of steps leading up to the pillared entrance there. In front of the steps stood a car which they both recognized as the Rolls-Royce tourer that had once belonged to the old Earl, and that was now the property of his son, Lord Garvald; but there was no sign of Garvald himself, nor of his chauffeur, and with her gaze skimming the entrance steps, Jinty remarked,

"Garvald's well ahead of us, it seems."

"I told you to call him the Earl of Ballinford now," her mother reminded her; but Jinty did not hear this. A voice in her mind, the rasping voice of the old Earl, was shouting, *"You know bloody well that Garvald's not allowed to drive this car, or any other!"* and she went up the steps with a picture of the old Earl's face in her mind—craggy, brick-red, arrogant, with eyes of a pale and icy blue—the kind of face she had once imagined for a pirate, or perhaps a robber chief. And the curious thing there, of course, was that—even although she had been small at the time—she had been right in her imagining! To win a title and lands in the first place, according to Archie Meikle, you just had to prove yourself stronger and be a bigger robber than the rest, and

7

the Ballinfords had been no better than anyone else when it came to that sort of thing.

"Jinty!" her mother's voice came. "You're dreaming again. You'll get lost in this place if you dawdle behind like that."

That was true. The Sheriff Court Building held a maze of corridors, long, dim, and high-ceilinged. Steps led upwards into further dimness, and the whole place seemed to have a life of its own that took no account of outsiders like themselves. Doors stood open. There were the sounds of telephones ringing and typewriters clacking. Clerks hurried from room to room with papers in their hands. Policemen stood around looking majestic, or came treading heavily past. When it began to seem as if they might wander around forever, her mother finally asked a direction of one of these policemen, and he led them to a door that had a big brass nameplate with *PROCURATOR FISCAL* engraved in flowing script on it. A woman clerk came to their knock on this door, and told them,

"I'm afraid you'll have to wait. The Fiscal's been delayed in Court this morning."

Smiling apologetically, she showed them through the open door of the room that faced the office with the brass nameplate. Lord Garvald was in this other room, seated on one of the straight, dark-colored chairs ranged around its walls. Archie Meikle sat in another of the chairs, a little distance from Lord Garvald. The woman clerk gave another apologetic smile all around, and went away, leaving the door of the room still open behind her. Lord Garvald inclined his head and wished them "Good morning." Archie Meikle did the same, but it was only Jinty who answered Archie's greeting.

"Sit here," her mother told her, taking up a position opposite the open door; and as Jinty sat down, still feeling the embarrassment of that unanswered "Good morning," she wondered if her mother would ever forgive Archie Meikle. It wasn't likely, she thought—not when her mother hadn't even forgiven Meg!

There were no magazines in the room, nothing to look at except the buff envelope in her hands and the other people seated there. Her mother's face had the kind of look it showed often during the winter when money was short and they had begun owing at the village store—a tight, buttoned-down look of grim endurance. Lord Garvald sat with his arms folded and one leg crossed over the other—very elegant in his Savile Row suit and the handmade leather shoes that were polished to a mirror-brightness. He was staring straight ahead of him, the back of his head leaning against the dull brown of the wood panelling the walls of the room. He was very like the old Earl, except that he was pale, and he was too young yet for his features to have that craggy, weathered look.

Archie Meikle was leaning right forward in his chair, head bent, elbows on spread knees, and hands dangling down between them, his eyes fixed on the patch of floor at his feet. In the dim atmosphere of the room his swarthy face looked even darker than usual. The lock of black hair that always fell over his forehead when

9

he was working at the forge had been slicked into place with some oily kind of hairdressing. He was wearing his best suit, his Sunday-go-to-meeting one—except, of course, that Archie never went to church—and the muscles of his shoulders were straining the seams of it almost to bursting point. Beside the fairness and the tall, slim elegance of Lord Garvald, Jinty thought, he looked like a dark and powerful gnome—just like he did when he was working in the smithy opposite his own tall, fair son, Tom.

A rush of footsteps in the corridor made them all glance quickly towards the door. A man poked his head into the room, a small thin man with a lawyer's black gown drooping from his shoulders. He smiled vaguely and withdrew, coming face to face as he did so with the woman clerk who had shown them where to wait. The clerk had a long sheet of paper in her hand, and he took this from her. Some words came out of the muttered conversation they had over it.

". . . *Ballinford   case . . . important . . . correct order   of   interview . . .*"

Jinty's mother nodded towards the man in the lawyer's gown. "That's him," she whispered. "Mr. Talbot, the Procurator Fiscal."

The woman clerk came towards the waiting room. The Fiscal hurried into his office. The clerk read from her paper, "The Earl of Ballinford," and then said,

"If you would come this way, please. Mr. Talbot's sorry you've been kept waiting, but he'll see you now."

With one hand she indicated the Fiscal's office, and

Lord Garvald—"the present Earl," Jinty corrected her own thought—went towards it.

"One of us is in for a long wait," Archie Meikle said resignedly. Nobody answered him, and as the door of the Fiscal's office opened to admit Lord Garvald, Archie resumed his elbows-on-knees position. Jinty arranged her feet evenly side by side on the floor, squaring off their position in much the same way as she was trying to square off her thoughts of what *she* would have to tell Mr. Talbot. But somehow the thoughts wouldn't allow themselves to be tidied up like that. Somehow they kept darting all over the place, back and forwards over all the years she had known the old Earl; and suddenly she found herself remembering how long Archie Meikle had known him. All his life, they said, the whole lifetimes of both men—which meant that the Earl couldn't really have been so old, because Archie was— what? Fifty-five? Sixty?

Unaware of how she had begun to stare again at Archie while she made her calculations, she saw him lift his head in the way that a person does when he feels another's eyes on him. He looked puzzled for a moment when he caught the intentness of her expression; then he winked at her, and grinned.

Involuntarily, as she had done so often in the past, Jinty returned his grin; and on the instant, as if the familiar interchange had sparked off some steadying influence in her mind, all those darting thoughts were focussed on the event she needed to recall most clearly before she came face to face with the Procurator Fiscal.

The first occasion of hearing about the Ballinford doom—that was what she had to remember now, in every detail. And Archie Meikle's smithy was the place for that! If she could picture the smithy and imagine herself there now, she realized, she would be able to put everything else connected with the Earl's death into its proper order. Then she could begin to decide how much—or how little—to say when the Fiscal questioned her about it!

With a sense of discovery quickening her heartbeat, she leaned back in her chair and began letting her mind take her back to the old, familiar occupation that had always been a favorite with her—standing in the doorway of the smithy, watching Archie and Tom Meikle at work there.

2

The transition from the Fiscal's waiting room was made, and she was back to one of those many occasions when she had stood there in the smithy doorway. Behind her now, was the smithy yard. At the end of the lane leading from one side of the yard, was the village school where Miss Carson would be ready to give her a belting if she was late again for class. And now that she had all that pictured clearly in her mind, she could visualize Archie, too, swinging his fourteen-pound hammer down with a force that sent sparks shooting from the anvil, then—just as he had done a moment before in the waiting room—looking up to wink and grin at her.

With the remembered impulse to wink and grin in reply then, came also the thought that she had always liked Archie Meikle. He was an atheist, of course, "a right godless creature," according to Mr. Elphinston, the minister, but that wasn't something that bothered

her; and once she had stopped at the smithy doorway
she never cared whether or not she was late for school.
For a start, there was the forge fire, roaring in showers
of red and gold sparks up the vast black throat of the
chimney sloping away from the raised stone hearth
heaped with glowing charcoal. And if she lingered long
enough in her fascination with the sparks, Archie sometimes let her pump the big wooden handle of the bellows
that kept the fire going at the right heat—a privi-
lege that was only allowed, as a rule, to the boys of the
village.

Then there was the pattern of sounds that Tom and
Archie played with their hammers on the big and the
little anvils standing in front of the fire—first a series
of small taps, followed by one great blow on the piece
of red-hot iron that was being shaped, then a shorter
series of the small taps to finish off each separate part
of the pattern. Archie worked with his back bent right
down over the anvil, his big hooked nose seeming
almost to be sniffing the iron; and, hunched like this,
his gnomelike figure looked more than ever powerful.
Tom Meikle stood with only his head bent. Tom's
height, and his fairness made him look like a young
Viking, and there was an easy grace about everything
he did; but all of Archie's actions were forceful, and he
was impatient.

When Archie had to wait in front of the fire for a
piece of iron to heat, he jigged about from one foot to
the other all the time, and sweat glowed in great drops
on his dark face. When Tom held a piece of iron in the

forge, he stood with his hands steadily gripping the pincers that held it, and the only movement about him was the flicker of the fire over the little golden hairs on his extended arms.

There was nearly always something going on at the smithy, too, apart from the work; nearly always talk of some kind to be heard; for the smithy was the great meeting place for all the men of the village, and it was when they got together like that, that she could hear the really good talk about everything from politics to potatoes. And that was especially so when her own Dad happened to be there, because—in spite of being just an odd-job man on the Earl's estate—he could still talk like a book on any subject under the sun.

What was more, there wasn't a living thing on the estate had a secret from him. He knew where the owls nested, and where the roe deer lay up by day, where the otters played with their young by the river, and where the badgers roamed by night. He even knew odd things such as how blue-tits taught their nestlings to fly—by edging them along a branch, he said, and then pushing them off the end of it! That was true, he swore. He had seen a pair of parent blue-tits at it. And through the other men's laughter, he demonstrated how it had been done.

There was a great sense of importance, somehow, in being there when the men talked like that, even although she knew her mother's opinion of it all. "Time-wasting," her mother called it. The smithy was the biggest time-waster ever invented, according to her,

15

and the other women in the village agreed with that. If they had something to be mended, they either sent it to the smithy or just went in and out again—all except Mrs. Torrie, that is. Mrs. Torrie was the wife of Alec Torrie, the plowman at Ballinford Mains; and even although she was small, and fat, and gap-toothed, she was still convinced of her fatal charm for men. She enjoyed lingering in the smithy; and when she did, she raised quite a different sort of laugh—like the day she had brought Archie a pair of fire tongs to be mended, teetering into the smithy on the tiny, high-heeled shoes that carried her so unsteadily through the muck at the Mains, and coyly smiling her wide, gap-toothed smile at him until he was in more of a sweat than ever.

"That Torrie woman," he said when she had gone, "is a classical case of the disease they call delusions of glamour."

"There's no such thing," Tom told him. "The disease you're thinking of is paranoia—delusions of grandeur."

"For God's sake, man!" Archie roared. "It was a play on words, wasn't it? A joke, a joke! But it would need a nail and a hammer, it seems, to get a joke into your brain."

"Is that so?" Tom asked. "Well, it proves that Johnson was right, after all, I suppose."

"Johnson? Johnson?" Archie demanded. "Who's he? What's he got to do with it?"

"Dr. Johnson," Tom said calmly. "The famous eighteenth century lexicographer and wit, Dr. Samuel Johnson. According to him, it required a surgical operation to get a joke into a Scotsman's head."

Tom was grinning by that time; and by that time, too, Archie could see that the joke was now at his expense. But he took it in good part. He always did, when Tom tripped him up like that, because—ever since Mrs. Meikle had died, years ago—they'd had no one at all except one another; and as well as being fond of him, Archie was also secretly very proud of having a son who was so well-read as Tom. But in spite of the deep books that Tom could quote, Archie still knew a lot more about certain things than he did—especially when it came to long-ago village matters that were the kind of thing you couldn't find in any book. And it was from Archie, of course, that she had first heard of the one that proved to be the most important of them all—the Ballinford doom.

The old Earl had called into the smithy on the day that had happened. He often came there to talk to Archie, and in one way that made sense because—again according to Mr. Elphinston, the minister—each was as godless as the other. But, in another way, it didn't. The Earl was an aristocrat, and a true-blue Tory. Archie was the village blacksmith, and a Socialist; and neither was afraid to shout his views from the housetops.

"You lot," Archie was fond of telling the Earl, "you're just parasites on the body politic. Just the lingering remnants of a feudal society, that's all you are."

"And what's wrong with bloody feudalism?" the Earl

would roar then. "You were glad enough for our lot to lead you in the Great World War—or in any war, come to that."

"Aye, and what's war but a fight between one bloody capitalist and another? When did the poor of the world ever benefit from war?"

Archie's answer always came back in a roar just as loud, and that would be the two of them launched into a real hammer-and-tongs battle of words. Yet still there were other occasions when they talked together of past times in the village, of the fights they had had as boys and the skylarks they had got up to then, of Archie's craft, of the great plowing championships there had been when they were both young men, and of the way the old breed of Clydesdale horse for the plowing was dying out; and it was when they talked like this that she could sense a friendship where the roots went deep and that was based on a curious kind of respect for one another.

It was after conversations like these, too, that the pair of them were likely to get roaring drunk together in the bar of *The Black Bull*—but that, again, didn't make sense, because everybody else looked askance at Archie for contradicting himself so far as to hobnob with the Earl one day and blast him for an aristocrat the next. And so far as the Earl was concerned also, the drinking bouts with Archie were just one more thing to add to the reputation that meant people speaking of him sometimes as "the bad old Earl."

All of this and a lot more besides had flashed through

her head on that same day of hearing about the Ballin-ford doom—the day her eleven-year-old self had come racing from school towards the smithy, only to be halted by the sight of the Earl's Rolls-Royce in the street outside the smithy yard. John Ferguson, the chauffeur, was at the wheel. A glance inside the smithy itself showed her the Earl deep in conversation with Archie Meikle. There was no sign of Tom Meikle; but, as she stood debating with herself whether to stay or to go, she glimpsed Tom through the open doorway of the shed where he spent a lot of time tinkering with cars. A second later he was joined by another figure—John Ferguson's son, Dave—and that decided her.

Dave Ferguson was crazy about cars—already talk-ing about setting up his own garage although he was still just sixteen, and once he and Tom Meikle got to-gether there was no telling how long they would be. The forge fire was low, too, which was another reason for thinking there was no point in her lingering further. And what was more, it was clear from the earnest way the Earl and Archie were talking that no work would be done for a while yet.

"I'm warning you, you're a fool to ask Elphinston's advice on it." That was all she heard of Archie's side of the conversation. And then, just as she turned away from the smithy door, the Earl answered,

"But goddammit, Archie, Garvald's eighteen now. How much longer can I go on keeping him wrapped in cotton wool?"

With thoughts of her own affairs now crowding in so

that this registered only vaguely on her mind, she went across the smithy yard and into the street. For a moment or two she dallied there, looking absently across it to the harvesters at work on the fields of barley standing opposite; then suddenly coming to a decision on those crowding thoughts, she ran on down the street, past her own home and up the rise that led to the church.

The gate of the churchyard was open. She slipped through it, and started weaving a way among the tombstones towards the very oldest part of the churchyard. This was where the tombs of the Crusading knights lay, on a stretch of ground overgrown thickly with soft moss that held the press of her steps like footprints in deep green snow, and this was where she halted.

There were five of the tombs, each one forming a waist-high rectangular plinth for a flat slab on which lay the life-size figure of a knight carved in stone. The feet of each of these figures rested on the carved shape of a small dog. Stone arms were bent upwards across the chest to let the hands come together in prayer. The heads were helmeted in stone, the bodies covered in stone armor. There was a dagger at the belt around each waist. Great stone swords lay quiet by their masters' sides; and as she stood staring at all this, she was thinking of the village, and dragons, and Miss Carson.

The village was old—so old that, when she was small, the fact of the knights' tombs had made her think it must have been there since the day of dragons. And it was this, of course, that had surfaced from her daydreaming in the middle of Miss Carson's history lesson, because her mind had been wandering back to that early belief when the voice snapped at her,

"What time have I been talking about, Janet Morrison?"

"The day of dragons, miss." With horror she had heard the words coming from herself; and then there had been sniggering from the rest of the class while she excused herself to Miss Carson and tried to explain how she had come to say such a thing.

"For a girl in her twelfth year," Miss Carson said grimly, "you have a remarkably childish mind." She turned to the rest of the class then, and told them,

"The stone figures we have just heard about are effigies of the Crusading knights who were ancestors of your local landowner, the Earl of Ballinford. It was these knights also, who successively built the castle and small private chapel standing now in ruined form only on the summit of Temple Rock, the crag which overlooks the site of the present Ballinford Hall. That is more than enough to place them firmly in the realm of fact. But the dragon, kindly note, is a mythical animal."

Miss Carson had eyes like brown buttons. Her nose was like a small white button. She enjoyed explaining things, and when she was enjoying herself the brown buttons shone and the nostrils of the white button flared and twitched. She chalked rapidly on the blackboard until she had her sentence about the dragon written there. Then she rapped the tip of her long pointer under each word and repeated firmly,

"Mythical. A mythical animal. Is that clear, Janet?"

Miss Carson never used pet names like "Jinty," but she was a good teacher. She destroyed illusions. That, she explained to the class, was what teaching was all about, especially where they themselves were concerned. This was Scotland in the year 1932 and unemployment was rife in the land, which meant that they must all learn to put childish fantasies in their proper place and keep their minds on facts. It was no excuse, therefore, for Janet Morrison to say she had been daydreaming of connecting the imaginary time of dragons with the stone knights in the churchyard, because a girl who allowed her mind to wander like that would never learn anything worthwhile.

"And then," she asked, "where will you be, Janet, in the competition for jobs?"

There wasn't any answer to that kind of question, and even if there had been, she was too embarrassed to attempt it. And yet, in spite of that, in spite of knowing how right Miss Carson was about everything, she had still found herself vaguely regretting the final loss of all her splendid, long-ago ideas about dragons that soared and breathed flame. And along with this, as she had come out of school that day, there had been a sort of resentment at the lecture about the knights themselves.

You couldn't belong to the village, after all, and still not know they were the Earl's ancestors; and if Miss Carson herself hadn't been fairly new to the place, she would have realized that. What was more—and this was the thing that had finally sent her running from

the smithy up to the churchyard—she was sure there was a certain something about the knights that didn't fit in anywhere with the practical way Miss Carson talked. She studied them again, trying to think what this might be.

Their color was dark gray, almost black, and time had weathered them until their faces were just featureless shapes. The praying hands were peaceful, and yet— The answer to that puzzling something flashed suddenly into her mind. It was the contradiction between those praying hands and the weapons they had once employed. And now she had realized that, it seemed that the knights were not truly peaceful—and not truly at rest either! Instead of that, she felt, there was a sort of leashed force about them, as if each one lay there alert for some signal that would set him rising from his slab to stalk in gray ghostliness through the grayness of the old churchyard, the ghost of a little dog running at his heels and the stone sword drawn at last for some fearful, unnameable purpose.

A spasm of sheer terror at the very idea of this made her turn quickly away from the tombstones, and in the same moment she heard a voice booming loud and close to her,

"The wages of sin is death!"

With her moment of terror almost becoming panic at this, she swung round to hunt for the source of the words, and saw two men approaching her. One of them was Mr. Elphinston, and as soon as she became aware of this she realized it was he who had spoken. Mr.

Elphinston had a most powerful voice, in spite of being such a thin, shrunken creature. The figure towering tall and broad at his side was the Earl, and following hard on that realization came the moment when she actually did panic.

Partly, she knew afterwards, it was simply embarrassment at the thought of being asked what she was doing in the churchyard on a schoolday. But there was more to it than that. Deep in her heart, from the time as a small child when she had first heard him called "the bad old Earl," she was afraid of the Earl of Ballinford. The moment's fantasy about the knights had unnerved her enough to allow a sudden surfacing of this fear, and it was in panic reaction from it that she ducked down to hide herself in the shelter of one of the knights' tombs.

"You seem very sure of that, minister." The two men had continued talking as they walked, and that was the Earl's voice she heard as she slid down to press herself against the tomb.

"I have the authority of the Bible for it," Mr. Elphinston boomed; and added confidently, "Paul's Epistle to the Romans, Chapter six, Verse twenty-three."

"I'll cap that," the Earl said instantly, "and from the same Epistle. '*In death there is no sin.*' What d'ye say to that, minister?"

The two men were level with her now, and only a few feet away. She could see the Earl's brick-red face with its bristling mustache that was the same pepper-

and-salt color as his hair, but at that moment there was something else, apart from arrogance, in its craggy lines; an expression she had never seen before in the icily blue eyes.

"I say that the Devil can quote Scripture for his own ends." Swiftly Mr. Elphinston took up the challenge in the Earl's question; and just as swiftly, the Earl struck back at him.

"The Devil is also called the Earl of Hell, sir, and I've a few sins yet to commit before you give me that title instead of my own."

Both men passed out of her view then, with Mr. Elphinston answering, "Don't play with words. You can't deny the sins you do commit—drink, gambling— not to mention the way you've openly flaunted Lady Dorothy as your mistress all those years since your wife died. As for the spendthrift ways that have made you a byword in the county—"

The accusing voice of the minister died away into nothing, at this point. In the total silence that followed, she waited to see what might happen next, and from the street outside the churchyard came eventually a sound that she took to be the engine of the Earl's car coming to life. That, too, died again into nothing, and when this further silence had endured a few moments longer, she rose cautiously to survey the churchyard. Once more she discovered she was alone there; but it was the Earl now, who occupied her mind. And, she decided, it was not what he had said that had impressed her. It was the bitter way he had spoken, and the tormented, protesting something she had seen lurking in the accustomed arrogance of his face.

In the sight of this lingering then on her inward vision, she sensed this something as a sort of power, yet still a power that was locked in and desperate; and groping for words to define this to herself, she connected it with that feeling of leashed and hidden force she had got from the knights who were his ancestors. It had something to do with death, she realized then; yet it also had something very much to do with being alive.

A shiver passed over her at this thought, and for a moment she was gripped by the feeling of foreboding she had heard her father talk of as "fey." Yet even in spite of this, she continued to be fascinated by the thought that had inspired the fey feeling, and could not understand why this should be so. Broodingly she began to retrace her steps through the churchyard, and it was in the course of this that another connection clicked into place in her mind.

"—you're a fool to ask Elphinston's advice—"

"The smithy!" she thought then. "I'll ask Archie Meikle."

Running now, she passed through the gate and into the street, but halfway back to the smithy door, she remembered Archie's attitude to youngsters who overheard talk there. Anything they picked up in his smithy, he maintained, was no more than they might normally pick up anywhere. But he wasn't in business to educate kids in the facts of life, and outright questions on gossip that didn't concern them was another matter. Her steps slowed; and once eventually back at the smithy door again, she stood for quite a while looking in at what was going on there, but still saying nothing. Tom Meikle was there now, as well as Archie, and she wondered if that was because Dave Ferguson had had to leave when his father drove the Earl's Rolls down to the churchyard.

"You're quiet the day, Jinty." It was Tom, as it happened, who challenged her silence at last; and hesitantly she answered,

"It's just that—Well, I'm thinking about something."

"A dangerous business, thinking," Archie joked; and Tom asked teasingly,

"How would you know that, Dad?"

That was enough to set the two of them off on one of their sparring matches, she realized, and doggedly began pursuing the opening Tom had given her.

"I was thinking. And what was in my mind was something Miss Carson said about the stone knights in the churchyard."

Tom's face took on a sudden interest at the mention of Miss Carson. "So you're in her class now, are you?" he remarked. "Well, you'll learn something there."

"Forbye that," Archie added slyly, "Marjorie Carson's a bonny lass—eh, Tom?"

Tom turned away, not answering this except by a reddening of the face that was due to more than the heat of the forge fire. Archie grinned at the way he had got his own back on Tom's teasing, and in the small silence this produced, she continued,

"Miss Carson spoke about the knights being the Earl's ancestors, and I went to look at them. Then Mr. Elphinston and the Earl came into the churchyard. I heard them arguing with one another, and there was something about the Earl—strange, like the feeling I got from the stone knights."

"What sort of a feeling was that?" Archie asked. He wasn't really interested. She could tell that by his tone; but it was different when she tried to explain the feeling to him. There was a look shot between him and Tom, then, and Archie asked her—a bit too casually, she noticed,

"Tell me, Jinty, have you ever heard talk of the Ballinford doom?"

She shook her head, her mouth open, eyes wide, at the sound of the words. Archie put down his hammer and said softly,

"My God!"

He looked at Tom and told him, "She's fey, Tom. I always said she was fey, and this proves it."

"You say too much sometimes," Tom remarked. His tone was disapproving, and she was afraid it would stop Archie saying any more to her. Quickly, she told him,

"It's all right, Mr. Meikle, I know what fey is. My Dad says that about me sometimes. But why should I feel fey about the Earl? And what's this Ballinford doom?"

Again there was that look between Tom and Archie.

Then Tom shrugged, and said,

"She'll hear talk of it sooner or later, I suppose."

Archie nodded to this. He went on hammering for another few moments—like he was hammering out the shape of what he had to say, she thought—and then he looked up at her.

"I'll tell you about the Ballinford doom," he said, "and then you can work out for yourself the reason for that feeling you got from the Earl. But first of all, Jinty, what were they arguing about—the Earl and the minister?"

"Sin," she told him. "Mr. Elphinston said, *'The wages of sin is death.'* They argued about that, and then Mr. Elphinston started to lecture the Earl about all his own sins."

"I knew it!" Archie exclaimed. He turned to Tom. "I warned him. I said, *'If you go to Elphinston for advice you'll get nothing but pious claptrap for your pains.'* But would he listen to me? Would he hell!"

"You can't blame the Earl for that," Tom objected. "He dotes on his son, after all. And that gives him the kind of problem that would make a man turn anywhere for help."

"But he knows what Elphinston's like." Archie objected. "He knows damned well he could as soon expect Christian understanding from my anvil as from that narrow-minded old tyrant."

The conversation was in danger of slipping away from her, she realized. Quickly, before Tom could answer this, she reminded Archie,

29

"You were going to tell me, Mr. Meikle. About the—about, you know, the Ballinford doom."

"Aye, so I was." Archie agreed. "Well, it's simple enough, Jinty. There's never yet been an eldest son of that family has lived to succeed his father. Wars, diseases, accidents—there's been a variety of causes for that. But whatever the cause, the result is always the same. The eldest son dies. A younger son succeeds to the title, lands, money—everything. That's been the way of it for hundreds of years now. That's the doom on the Ballinfords."

She couldn't make the connection at first—couldn't see how it related to the conversation she had overheard in the churchyard, or to the sense she had got there of something in the Earl that was very powerful, yet still locked in and desperate. Then, in a flash, she did see it.

"But—Hey, Mr. Meikle—!" she exclaimed, and then stopped, her nerve failing at the prospect of giving words to her realization. Archie guessed what was in her mind. He had gone back to his hammering, but he paused in it now at the sound of her exclamation, and looked up at her.

"That's right, Jinty," he told her. "The Earl hasn't got any son apart from Lord Garvald—never had, and never will have now. And if Mr. Elphinston's God won't take a hand in breaking the doom that hangs over that boy, I can't see any other way out of it. Not one that bears thinking about, at least!"

3

Archie wouldn't listen to a single one of the questions she wanted answered then. Did Lord Garvald himself know about the Ballinford doom—and if he did, who had told him? And what about the Earl and his older brother—the one who must have died so that he could *be* the Earl—how had the doom worked then? What sort of man had that brother been, and how had he died?

"Ask your own folk," Archie told her. "I've said all I'm going to say."

But there were still no answers to be had, even when she did get home that day. The bus that brought Meg and Linda from Haimston Academy had arrived by that time, but neither of them had ever heard of the Ballinford doom; nor, it seemed, were they the least interested in it. Meg had something quite different on her mind—something that made her impatient of talk about anything else; while Linda took her usual attitude of dismissal towards everything that wasn't either provable or useful.

"You're meddling with matters far beyond your age." That was her mother, hiding behind the sort of answer that older people always gave when they took it for granted that she couldn't grasp the way their minds worked. And even although her father was one of the few she could trust not to be like that, this was one time when he wasn't of any help either.

"If I were you," he advised, "I'd forget I ever heard about it. It's a right unhappy business, after all, and so what's the use of poking further into it?"

That was the other side of her father, the one that always slid away from facing any bother, and usually it annoyed her mother. But this time was different. This time her mother approved of his attitude, and it was the rest of what her mother had to say that finally put an end to all her questioning.

"And you're not to go around the village asking those sort of things, because I'll not have the folk here given any chance to say that someone in *my* family is gossiping about other people's business."

That was more than an order, she realized. If there was one thing her mother was hard on, it was gossiping— which made her words a warning also. And so, reluctantly, she allowed her knowledge of the Ballinford doom to slip to the back of her mind, not realizing—how could she, then?—the place it would have in all the other events linking her to the Earl, and her mother, and the trouble over Meg. Meg and the Paddy woman, Meg and Mrs. Torrie's diamond heels . . .

The thing Meg had her mind fixed on then was the kirn—the harvest celebration that was held every year on the upper floor of the big barn at Ballinford Mains. That was something all three of them, Meg and Linda, and herself, had always wanted to see, but this was especially so with Meg. Ever since she was little, Meg had been fascinated by the thought of it. But the kirn, their mother said, was nothing more nor less than a pagan riot, with whooping and skelloching and dancing till all hours of the night.

Beer was drunk there; and beer, she told them, was the devil's brew. As for the rest of what went on at the kirn, with couples slipping away into the dark and then coming back with guilty looks on their faces, that was another good reason why *her* girls would never be part of such an affair. And that was something they'd better mind too, if they were ever going to make anything of themselves instead of spoiling their chances at the start by getting mixed up with a lot of village louts.

"Make something of yourselves!" It was her constant cry to them, with all sorts of examples of how her own folk had made themselves schoolmasters and doctors and lawyers and well-to-do merchants. It was all a part of the yearly lecture about the kirn, ever since Meg had first asked if they could join the other youngsters who were allowed to perch in the straw bales in the barn and watch what went on there. And maybe it was just because she went on about it so much that some of the first fantasy in their imaginings of it had stayed with them.

"Pagan Riot! Devil's Brew!" There was, said Linda, a wild and wanton ring to the very words she used about it, and they had all laughed at this. But that was later, of course; much later than the time when the attraction of these same words had drawn them to listen, open-mouthed, to the stories Mrs. Torrie told on the morning after each year's kirn. High jinks with paper streamers and balloons, fiddles shrilling, men's voices roaring out the words of the kirn-tunes, feet stamping in dances wild enough to raise a golden cloud of corn-dust from the barn floor—all these were part of Mrs. Torrie's stories and of the fantasy they had woven around the kirn; all these had been fuel to Meg's longing. And that year, Meg was nearly fifteen—old enough to go to the kirn and join in the dancing like all the other girls. But the way their mother thought about it, what hope was there of that?

"Just imagine it," Meg told Linda and herself after they had all listened in the usual silence to that year's lecture, "Tom Meikle, and Patie Anderson, and old Jake—all the chaps in the village, in fact, swilling down Devil's Brew and then stamping about in their tackety boots raising a Pagan Riot. We'd all really go to the bad if we saw that, wouldn't we?"

They were upstairs at the time in the attic bedroom shared among the three of them. It was late enough in the day for them to have lit the one candle they were allowed—it cost too much to burn electricity in bedrooms, their mother said—and Meg's face was clear in the candlelight. But it wasn't the face of bouncy cheerfulness that was usual with her. There was a flush on it. The mouth was drawn tight. The blue of the eyes glancing from Linda to herself had darkened to an almost violet color. This was Meg in one of her reckless moods, she realized; and out of all this, became suddenly aware of something she had never really thought about before.

Meg was beautiful! That was something she had always known, of course, especially on the many occasions when strangers had turned in the street with glances that skimmed over the mousey-brown heads of Linda and herself and came to rest admiringly on Meg's mass of golden-red hair. But it was still something she had always just accepted, in the same way as she accepted that Meg was bossy, and kindhearted, and noisy. And sometimes bold, too, in a way that could shake even Linda, who was only eleven months her junior and not the kind who was easily shaken. It was odd to be so suddenly and sharply aware of all this—odd, yet exciting too, as if she were getting the familiar feeling of Meg from the face of some lovely girl she had never seen before!

Linda was also staring at Meg, and Linda was uneasy. It showed in her face, and in her voice when she said,

"You're up to something, aren't you? The kirn— You're going to sneak out and go to it this year! Is that what's in your mind?"

Meg took her time about answering, and then she spoke slowly. "I'm going to ask," she told them. "Just one more time, I'm going to ask Mam for permission to go to it."

"But Meg"— Linda was exasperated now, instead of uneasy—"you know she'll refuse, just like she always has. And you know she'll get mad at you."

"Of course I know. But this time will be different, because this time I *won't* take no for an answer. I'll argue with her, try to make her see what it feels like for me to be the only one of my age that doesn't get to dance at the kirn."

"And if she won't see that?"

"I'll tell her I've got *rights!*" Meg sat up, arms straight by her sides, fists clenched. "It was different when I was small, because the kirn's a grown-up affair. But I'm as grown now as I'll ever be, and so I've a right to go to it. It's nearly three years, after all, since I—"

The flush on Meg's face grew suddenly deeper, as she hesitated there; and then, as if nerving herself to continue saying exactly what she had been thinking, she plunged on,

"—since I had the flowers."

It was the only phrase that any of them knew then, for menstruation—the country way of referring to it. It was also something they had been forbidden to discuss, so that they never had done so before then, except in furtive whispers; and Linda was immediately as embarrassed as Meg herself at this open mention of it. That was easy to see, in the way they looked away from one another and from herself. But it didn't affect her that way, of course, because the flowers was still just theory so far as she was concerned; and in the silence that fell on the other two, her mind was still busily pursuing thoughts of the kirn itself and the way that Mrs. Torrie's stories had chimed so marvelously with her own share in their early fantasies about it.

The Lancers! The Gay Gordons! The Dashing White Sergeant! It was from Mrs. Torrie she had first heard of all these—once, when she had been too small to recognize them as the titles of dances that were performed at the kirn, and she had thought instead that they were the names of young men; handsome young soldiers who came to dance with the girls there. The Dashing White Sergeant had been her favorite among them, too, and she had never quite got over the notion that you could actually meet him at the kirn, looking very tall, and dark, and handsome—and very dashing, of course, in his white uniform! Linda and Meg had begun talking again, and she broke into what Linda was saying, to ask,

"Meg, if Mam does say you can go, will you tell us all about it afterwards? And will you tell us if Mrs. Torrie really does cut a swathe among the men, the way she says she does?"

"You're an ass, Jinty," Meg told her; but she grinned, all the same, as she said this. They all grinned, because little Mrs. Torrie was so grotesque with her gappy yellow teeth and flyaway hair, and her shape was so much like a pillow tied in the middle that you really couldn't help being amused at her and her delusions of glamour.

"I wore my black and purple and gold, and I'm telling no lie, I was the belle of the ball."

That was always how she started all her accounts of the conquests she imagined she'd made at the kirn. But for the kirn, also, Mrs. Torrie always wore shoes with diamond heels, and they weren't imaginary. She had shown them the very shoes, tiny things, with narrow glittering spikes for heels—although she hadn't said whether the diamonds were real or not, of course. And, she had told them, the first time the Earl had danced with her in those shoes—as he did every year at the kirn—he had said to her,

"Mrs. Torrie, ma'am, you leap as nimble as a March hare in those heels, and I declare to God, there's not one of the fine ladies at Ballinford Hall can give me as much pleasure in the dance as you do."

Their grins turned into laughter as they reminded one another of all this, and Linda said, "The Earl might ask *you* to dance, Meg. And what'll you do if he pays you compliments like he does to Mrs. Torrie?"

"I'll decide once that happens," Meg said. And that put a stop to their laughter.

"You're still not serious about it—you can't be." Linda protested; and promptly Meg told her,

"I most certainly am, and I've got it all worked out too. Dad's not dead set against the kirn the way Mam is, and there can't be all that much wrong with it if he doesn't mind it. I'll get Dad to back me up."

Linda shrugged. "You'll be lucky! Dad isn't dead set

against anything—but he doesn't put up a fight for anything, either. That's why he never says a word about the kirn. And if you ask me, it's also why he's never there himself—although he probably would like to go. Peace at any price—that's Dad!"

It wasn't fair to talk like that about their Dad, even although it was true. He had been a good Dad to them, after all, in so many other ways. They all looked at one another knowing this, and with Linda already seeming a little ashamed.

"You've no business to sneer at him like that." Meg objected. "And anyway, I've got other ways of showing Mam that the kirn's nothing like as bad as she says it is. Names I could mention, for instance; names of respectable people who go there."

"Such as?"

Meg smiled the small triumphant smile of someone about to play a trump card, but it wasn't to Linda she spoke. Instead, she turned to say, "Such as your teacher, Jinty—Miss Carson."

"Miss *Carson!*" She could hear her own voice rising to a squeak of amazement as it echoed the name. "Miss Carson went to the kirn? How d'you know that?"

"Because," said Meg, "Dave Ferguson told me. Dave was there last year with his pal, Tom Meikle. And your Miss Carson, he said, had the time of her life dancing with Tom."

"And her a schoolteacher that's made something of herself," Linda exclaimed. "Dancing with the son of a blacksmith!"

Linda could mimic anybody. She was good at that, and the words came out in the very tones of their mother's voice, but Meg wasn't amused by this.

"Don't be daft," she retorted. "Tom Meikle's as well-read as any schoolteacher, and he's a nice fellow. Besides—" She checked herself there, but the rest of what she had been about to say hung on the air as clearly as if she had spoken it aloud. *Tom Meikle is big and fair, like a Viking. Tom Meikle is a handsome man.*

"Well, we'll see." Linda still wasn't convinced of anything Meg had said. "The kirn's not till tomorrow night and you've got till then to think it over. But I still say that Mam will just get mad at you—"

"Very likely," Meg interrupted, "but I'm ready for that."

"—and," Linda finished, "I don't believe you'll even dare to ask in the first place."

"That's just where you're wrong," Meg told her.

They got ready for bed then, with the other two still wrangling occasionally but with herself now thinking more about Miss Carson at the kirn than of Meg's determination to be there too. In school the next day she kept shooting curious looks at Miss Carson's straight, slim figure and trying to imagine her in a party dress, but it was hard to see her in anything except the school overall that was the same color as her brown-button eyes, and even harder to think of her neat bob of dark hair flying through the wild dances of the kirn.

"You haven't eaten much," their mother said to Meg

when supper was finished that night, and in a low voice Meg answered,

"I wasn't hungry."

Their father had started to sort out the materials he used for the wood carving that occupied him every winter, but he turned from this to give a glance of concern at her tone; and it was then that Meg asked permission to go to the kirn.

4

There was a brief, tense silence, then their mother said wearily, "Have I not told you—repeatedly told you—what I think of that affair?"

The echo of a sigh came from their father's fireside corner. "Have a bit of a heart, Jean," he coaxed. "It's only a once-a-year fling, after all."

Meg shot a grateful glance at him. "And other people go, Mam," she said. "Respectable people, like Jinty's teacher, Miss Carson."

"I'm not responsible for Miss Carson, Meg, but I do have a responsibility for you."

Their mother's voice had risen a tone by then, but still Meg persisted against the threat this implied. "And what about Dad?" she asked. "He doesn't talk about it the way you do, Mam. And surely it can't be as bad as you say it is if Dad doesn't mind it and if folk like Miss Carson go."

"Are you trying to tell me what's good and what's

bad—you, at your age?"

Meg began trying to answer this, but their mother's voice rushed on over her words.

"Your father, Miss Impudence, is a grown man who is entitled to his view—"

"And I'm fifteen come February," Meg interrupted. "That's old enough to know good from bad—or it is for me, anyway. And if I don't, I've a right to find out."

Their mother hissed on an indrawn breath of outrage. Her hand flashed out to slap against Meg's face—but even as Meg cried out at its impact, she was saying brokenly,

"Meg! Oh Meg, I didn't want—I—"

"For God's sake, wife!" A shout from their father drowned the stumbled words of regret, and he rose from his chair protesting, "That's no way to treat the lassie!"

Meg was crying now, one hand against her cheek where the slap had landed. Their mother turned from her. White-faced, her voice still shaking, she told their father,

"I'll thank you to let me control my own daughter."

There was a moment of dead silence, with the two of them face to face and staring hard at one another; then their father shrugged, and said in his normal, quiet voice,

"I can't argue your right to do that."

It seemed a reasonable enough answer, and so it was all the more surprising to see fiery color rush suddenly into the whiteness of their mother's face and to hear the breathless note of the voice that demanded,

"So that's the way you're thinking, is it? And after all these years of trying to tell me different!"

Meg turned and ran from the room. The sound of her feet clattering up the attic stairs echoed back to them. They all stood looking towards the sound, then their father said abruptly,

"You too, Linda. Away up to your room. And you, Jinty."

Thankfully, then, she followed Linda to the doorway leading to the stairs, and as soon as they were outside it, Linda said,

"Now what was the reason for all that? One minute it was all about Meg wanting to go to the kirn; and the next, there was Mam harking back to something that must have happened ages ago. It didn't make sense, did it?"

The door to the stairs opened behind them, and their father's voice called up, "Bed, all of you. And Meg, don't show yourself tomorrow till you're ready to make peace with your mother."

Their room was in darkness, with Meg sitting hunched beside the dressing table. Linda lit the candle, and turned with it in her hand to ask,

"Do *you* know, Meg? That row they suddenly started having over you—do you know what it was all about?"

Meg shook her head, then she sat up, wiping her eyes and saying in a choked voice,

"They used to fight like that over me when I was little. But they haven't done it since then and—oh, I can't really remember it much."

44

She turned towards them, her face coming into the light of the candle. There was no color in it except the red marks of fingers on one cheek. Her eyes blazed through the tears that still filled them.

"I didn't expect Mam to *hit* me," she said to Linda. "But she did—just like I was a kid with no sense."

"You went all the wrong way about it," Linda told her. "You rushed your fences, Meg, and it's your own fault you came a cropper."

Meg said nothing for a moment, then she muttered, "If she hadn't hit me—" Her glance went to the window of the room, and they guessed what she was thinking. The cherry tree outside the window had wide, spreading branches that made an easy route to the ground. Meg's glance came back into the room, and abruptly she announced,

"I'll give them an hour to settle down after all that row, and then I'll go out by the window."

"Meg!" Even although they had expected the decision, neither Linda nor herself could help exclaiming at the shock of hearing it actually spoken; but the alarm in their voices seemed only to bring back Meg's reckless mood.

"I said I've a right to go," she insisted. "And now I'll prove it."

"You'll be found out," Linda predicted. "Folk will guess you're there without permission, and someone'll tell Mam about it."

Meg shook her head. "That's not likely," she said; and when Linda challenged her to say why not, she went on,

"Because folk don't like the way Mam's view of the kirn puts *them* in the wrong over it. That's why there's not much chance of anyone running to tell her I was there."

"But that's not the only way you could be found out," Linda told her. "Suppose Mam looks out of the kitchen window, once you've gone. She can see the stairs on the outside of the barn from there—the ones you have to use to get to the upper floor. She might spot you going up them."

They were all getting ready for bed by that time. Meg didn't answer right away but waited until she had climbed into her own single bed. Then she looked across the few feet that separated her from Linda claiming her share of the double bed, and said,

"You know the Paddies?"

They did, of course. Everybody knew that the Paddies were the workers who came over from Ireland every year to pick the potato crop at Ballinford Mains. They waited to hear what Meg had to say about them, and she went on,

"And you know where they sleep—on the ground floor of the barn. Well, I'll go in by the door that gives onto their quarters. Then I'll climb up the ladder that's always left against the hatch opening onto the top floor where they have the kirn."

"You mightn't be able to open the hatch from below," Linda said. "The bolt's on the upper side of it, and you might find that the bolt's been shot."

Meg reached a hand to snuff out the candle. "It won't be," she said. But she would not tell Linda why she was so sure of this; and after that they all lay in silence, waiting, staring into the dark, and listening to small sounds from downstairs. The double bed grew cozy with the warmth of Linda and herself lying close together in it. She began drifting off to sleep, but a sudden flurry of movement from Linda jerked her wide awake again.

Linda was leaning out of bed to light the candle. Meg had plumped a couple of pillows under the cover of her own bed so that it looked as if she were still lying there. The rest of the house was very silent. Meg went to the closet to fetch her party dress. It was too short and too tight for her now, like all the other clothes from the previous year; but it was white, and the color suited her. She struggled into it, then sat down at the dressing table to brush her hair, and Linda said softly,

"Tell us, Meg. Why won't the hatch be bolted?"

Meg went on brushing her hair. The battered old mirror in front of her reflected an image so dim and distant that it was like a face seen in dreams; and in spite of the fact that she, too, wanted to hear the answer to Linda's question, it was this that really fascinated her now. The dream-Meg, it seemed to her then, was like some half remembered glimpse of the real Meg, and there was something in the thought that made her powerfully uneasy. The movement of the brush slowed, and stopped. The real Meg stood and turned to look at Linda, sitting up beside her in the double bed.

"The hatch won't be bolted," Meg said, "because Dave Ferguson said he'd make sure of that for me."

"Then you've planned it all along!" Linda exclaimed. "You meant to go tonight, no matter what Mam said."

Meg shook her head. "No, it wasn't like that," she said. "I wanted Mam's permission—I really did. And it was Dave's idea to leave the hatch open—just in case it turned out like this."

They stared at her, at the flushed face framed in the mass of shining hair, at the white dress gleaming in the candlelight. Meg turned to pick up her dancing shoes from where they lay on her bed. Beneath the white dress, the Wellington boots she needed to wear against the mud in the farm lane were two incongruous sticks of dusty black.

"Wish me luck," she threw over her shoulder at Linda. "You too, Jinty."

Beautiful Meg . . . The uneasy feeling grew too strong to be contained. Reckless—Meg was too reckless! "Don't go!" Now she was sitting up in bed with the uneasiness finding an urgent voice. "Please don't go, Meg!"

Meg looked at her, taken aback by that urgency. But it was only for a moment that this lasted, then Meg was smiling and telling her kindly,

"You can stop worrying, Jinty—really you can. Mam won't find out about me. I know how to take care of myself. And I'll have good fun!"

Dancing shoes in one hand, she reached with the other for the navy-blue school coat that would conceal her dress.

"Good luck," Linda said—envious now that the crunch had come. The tone of the words showed that and so did the wry little smile that went with them. Linda, she thought, always did have a last-minute envy of the chances that Meg took. But Meg was too excited to notice this now, and she herself was too disturbed to care about it. With her eyes on the dark-coated figure crossing to the attic window, she called softly,

"Good luck—oh, good luck, Meggie!"

"Thanks, Jinty. I'll tell you all about it later."

The answer came back to her muffled under the sound of the window sash being raised. Then Meg was leaning out to take her first grip on a branch of the cherry tree, pulling herself outwards till her figure merged with the darkness of the branch itself. Faint scrabbling sounds told of her climbing downwards from it. Linda shivered in the air from the open window. She pinched out the candle flame, and then burrowed down in bed, humping the blankets around her shoulders.

"I'm cold," she complained. "Cuddle me, Jinty, I'm cold."

Warmth began flowing between them as she cuddled into Linda's back; and presently, Linda asked,

"D'you suppose the Paddies will mind?"

"Mind what?"

"Meg going through their part of the barn, of course. D'you suppose they'll say anything to her?"

She thought of the Paddies as she had glimpsed them through the open door of the barn, crouching sullen and wary-eyed on the old potato sacks that were all they had for bedding. That look had alarmed her the first time she saw it, but when she had gone running to her father to tell him of it, he had said, "*Well, how d'you expect them to look, for goodness' sake—strangers in a strange land as they are?*" Then her mother had taken up the tale. "*And treated as they are too; because it's a shame and a disgrace to decency the way those poor Paddies are herded, men and women all together in that barn, with nothing but the bare floor to lie on and only one cold-water tap outside the barn for them to wash at.*"

"Well?" Linda kicked backward with her heel, impatient for an answer; and hastily, she said,

"No, they'll not mind."

The Paddies never did mind anything, she argued to herself. They weren't used to anything better than the way they lived in the barn—that was what the rest of the village said when her mother went on about how terrible it was for them. But even if they did mind, they wouldn't say anything to Meg. They were too scared of having their wages stopped to say a word out of place to anyone!

"Stay awake, Jinty!" Linda kicked backward again. "I want us both to be awake so we can ask Meg lots of questions when she gets back."

"She'll be a long time—maybe hours."

Linda turned to lie facing her. "Then stay awake for hours."

"All right, I'll try."

Lying with her eyes wide open on darkness, then, she let her mind drift away to imagined scenes of the kirn. Miss Carson, she thought; she had enjoyed herself last year with Tom Meikle for her partner. Would she be dancing with him again that night, and would her brown-button eyes be gleaming the way they did when she explained things in class? The Earl—she could see him dancing with Mrs. Torrie again; spiky diamond heels, smoothly-polished brown brogues rising and falling through the golden corn-dust. Mrs. Torrie said that the Earl never failed to dance with her. And Dave Ferguson—was it because he wanted to dance with Meg that he had left the hatch door open for her? Dave was handsome, too, but not like Tom Meikle.

Dave was like the Dashing White Sergeant, dark and slim, with a gallant sort of air. Meg in her gleaming white frock drifted across the darkness, smiling up at a white-uniformed young soldier who had Dave Ferguson's face. Then Meg started to cry, with one hand up to the place where her mother had struck her. All the other dancers became still, saying nothing, but frowning around in disapproval at her. They moved again, crowding in on her, still with those threatening frowns on their faces, and she stepped in front of Meg, trying to shout to them all to get back, get back; but her voice wouldn't come. Desperately she forced her throat to act, and woke with a sound that was no more than a squeak coming from it.

Linda was asleep, lying on her back and gently snoring. Still shivering in the aftermath of her dream she glanced from the sleeping face to the window, and tried to decide how long she herself had been asleep. An hour, perhaps? It was too dark for her to see the hands of the bedside clock; but it would take an hour, surely, for Linda to fall so deeply asleep that she was snoring? Faint sounds from outside the window caught her attention and sent sudden fear through her. Roughly she shook Linda awake. A hand appeared over the windowsill. Meg's head rose darkly into view. Then Linda sat up beside her, and Meg came over the sill. Wellingtoned feet thudded onto the floor; then Meg was padding towards them and speaking as she came, in a high, strange voice. Her figure loomed darkly over the double bed. Linda and she half rose to meet it; and then it came again, that high voice,

"I saw a baby born!"

Silence, then—a silence that throbbed with shock and unspeakable questions; and after a moment, her own voice sounding in a terrified whimper,

"I want the light! Put the light on!"

Meg didn't move. Linda leaned over to the bedside table and fumbled with the matches. Her hands were so unsteady that she had difficulty in striking a light; but at the third attempt, she did manage it. The candle wavered into life, and Meg sat down heavily on the edge of their bed. She was in a terrible state, they saw then, the front of her dress covered with mud, tears streaking a way through the mud spattered on her face; and yet, as the light on their bedside clock now also showed them, she had been gone even less than an hour.

"What on earth—!" Linda exclaimed. "How could you do that to yourself at the kirn?"

spoken before, she added,

"But maybe it's not too late yet."

She looked towards the door of their room as she spoke; and, just as they had done earlier, they guessed immediately what was in her mind. Downstairs, there was still hope for the Paddy woman. Downstairs was their father, who could get Mrs. Armitage, the postmistress, to phone for the doctor; and their mother, who was always the one to be called out to help at births until the doctor could come.

"But Meg," Linda protested, "you can't tell Mam about the Paddy woman without saying you saw her on your way to the kirn. And why should you take the blame for that when you didn't have any of the fun of it after all?"

"Because—" Meg began hesitantly, and then went on with the words rushing from her, "because I have to. Because a lot's happened to me since I went out to the kirn—a lot more than you think, and there's nothing else I *can* do now. That's why."

Linda shrugged. "Well, if you must, then I suppose you must. But I'm warning you, Meg. If you go down there now, Mam'll take the hide off you."

"I know that. But first of all she'll go out to help the Paddy woman."

Meg rose from the bed as she spoke and then began moving towards the door—slowly, with uncertain steps that made her look like someone just learning how to walk. Linda kneeled up in bed and called after her,

56

"I never got to the kirn after all," Meg said. "I went into the Paddies' quarters to climb the ladder to the trapdoor, like I said I would; but they were all awake and moving about. They stared at me. They wouldn't move out of the way when I tried to get through them to reach the ladder. Then I saw why. One of the Paddy women was lying on some potato sacks piled up near the foot of the ladder. And she was having a baby. They only had candles in the barn, and the woman that was bringing the baby out kept cursing and saying she couldn't see what she was after at all. *'Holy Mother of God, I can't see what I'm after at all'*—just like that she said it."

The room began to echo with sounds—strange, frightening sounds like the ones that came from the byre when one of the pedigreed cows was having difficulty in birthing a calf—*or was it only in her own mind that the noises existed?* She fought her way through their blurring impact, stammering questions as she did so.

"Did it—did it hurt the Paddy woman? Was it like the—the pedigree cattle?"

"I don't know," Meg said. "She didn't make a noise the way they do. She just sort of grunted sometimes. But she was crying, too. All the time, she was sobbing and crying something terrible."

"The doctor?" Linda asked shakily. "Why didn't they send for the doctor?"

Meg began to weep again. "I said that—I said that to them. There was blood all over the place but they said

53

they hadn't any money till they got paid at the end of the potato work, and the doctor wouldn't come without the money."

"But he would, he would!" Linda protested. "He came to Jinty when we didn't have any money, and he said to Mam, 'That's all right, you can pay me another time.'"

"I know that." Meg sobbed. "I told them so, but they wouldn't believe me. I argued and argued with them, but they just kept saying that the doctor was gentry, and wouldn't be bothered with the likes of them. They sent for the priest. I think she's dying because of them sending for the priest, and the blood, and the way they were all kneeling round her praying with their rosaries—those bead-things they have."

Meg's weeping had grown so convulsive by this time that they could hardly make out her last words. They exchanged looks over her bent head, then Linda too, began to weep; but she herself couldn't do that. Her mind had been caught, transfixed in horror by a sudden vision of the Earl and Mrs. Torrie in their annual caper at the kirn—the Earl and Mrs. Torrie dancing on the floorboards above the dying Paddy woman, diamond heels click-clicking, polished brogues thudding; Mrs. Torrie, fat and flaunting in her black and purple and gold, simpering her gap-toothed smile up at the Earl, and he with his arrogant robber-chief face grinning down at her. And all the time beneath them, the kneeling figures telling their rosaries and the life's

54

blood of the Paddy woman seeping away into the o potato sacks . . .

Revolted, she buried her face in her hands; but sti behind the squeezed-shut eyelids pressed hard by he fingertips, the two of them cavorted in monstrous enjoy ment. In despair, she looked up to cry.

"Why didn't you go for help?" And Linda echoed, "Yes, why didn't you?"

Meg's sobbing had tailed away by this time, but she was still shaking all over; her hands, her face, her whole body, all in a continuous tremble. Through long, shuddering breaths, she said,

"What makes you think I didn't try? But they were like sheep crowded around that ladder, and I couldn't make them understand they had only to let me climb it to get hold of someone at the kirn to help the woman. You know what they're like—they hardly even speak the same language as we do. And so then I ran to the top door into the barn—the one at the head of the outside steps. But it was shut—bolted on the inside; and there was such a racket going on at the kirn that nobody heard me rattling and banging away there. And then I—Well, I was just so upset I didn't seem to be able to think properly any more. All I wanted to do was to run, to get back home; but I fell in the lane, and that seemed to make everything even worse than before."

She took more long breaths, quieter ones, that finally brought her shaking under control; and then, in a voice that sounded strangely calm after the way she had

55

"Meg! Suppose the Paddy woman's already dead. It wouldn't be worth it then, would it?"

Meg stopped in her tracks to ask, "And supposing she isn't?"

There was no answer from Linda; and, still moving with those uncertain, learner's steps, Meg went downstairs.

5

The sudden vision of that night stayed printed on her mind. She couldn't get rid of it. And Mrs. Torrie wasn't funny any more. She was a monster. The Earl too. They were both monsters!

The Paddy woman died. The baby died too. In spite of Dad rousing Mrs. Armitage and getting a phone call through to the doctor, in spite of Mam hurrying as hard as she could down to the barn with the midwife's bag always kept ready behind the door of their house, the Paddy woman was dead by the time she got there; and as for the baby, it lasted for no more than minutes after the doctor managed to get it to the hospital.

The priest the Paddies had sent for came to their house, and all the time she watched him sitting there, it wasn't his pale, severe face she saw, nor the black cassock that would have seemed so strangely papist to her at other times. It was still the dance of death. The monsters were still there in her mind, and the Earl was looming larger and larger in her vision of them. She listened to her father talking to the priest, trying to answer all the questions the man had to ask.

"There's a contract system for that Irish labor, you see. They hire themselves out in gangs, through a contractor; but they're poor, ignorant souls, after all, and a lot of these contractor fellows work a real racket with them. They get the contract money from the farmer, but they don't give the Paddies the proper share of it that's due to them as wages; and even that, they don't get till the end of the season. That's why they never have any decent accommodation—they can't afford it. And so it's a kindness, really, for the farmer to let them use the barn—terrible as the conditions there are for them."

But it was the Earl who owned the barn, the farm, the land, the estate, power, money—everything. Why didn't he put a stop to it? How could he let such things happen if he wasn't a monster?

"But there's an ultimate responsibility, surely?" the priest said. "The owner of the estate—he could control the terms of the contract."

Carefully her father laid down the small piece of wood he had been whittling into the shape of a deer. Then, with his shoulders rising in a shrug of question, he said, "Tell me how. The same system rules all over the country, and it's got deep roots. The contractors move from county to county, and the labor goes from farm to farm. How can one owner change it all? And besides, it's just another part of the estate management;

59

and it's Mr. Gillan, the Earl's factor, who looks after that."

Nothing of this made any difference. The dance went on. The robber-chief face still grinned. The monster was there in her mind. She saw the priest's eyes on her before he asked,

"Is that child always so white?"

"I'm all right," she said quickly, and bent down with a quick pretense of tightening her shoelace, so that no one else could notice her color. The priest asked where Meg was. He wanted to speak to Meg about the Paddy woman; but her mother said stiffly,

"My daughter is forbidden to discuss the matter."

The priest had to go away then, and that was the end of it for him—except for any gossip he could pick up in the village, of course. And what with Mrs. Armitage having listened in to the phone call the way she always did, and people putting two and two together to fill in the gaps of the story she told, there was a terrible amount of that! But it still wasn't the end of it for Meg, or for herself either, because it wasn't only what Meg had done on the night of the kirn that mattered eventually. It was all the things that followed from it, and from Meg's punishment for that night.

Meg was not to have a single evening out for the rest of that year, they were told—positively none at all, not even to something so harmless as a church social. That was to be the main part of her punishment. But on top of that, the usual Saturday afternoon shopping trips to Haimston were now also banned to all three of them, because—their mother said—they had all connived at Meg's wrongdoing, and so they must all share at least partly in the punishment for it.

Linda was really annoyed about this, and all the more so when she discovered that Meg meant to give away nothing at all of what had been said between their mother and herself on the night of the kirn.

"That's my business," she insisted calmly. And to their surprise, she was just as calm over the whole of her punishment. The only thing that seemed to be able to upset her at all, in fact, was any mention of the Paddy woman and her baby dying after all, in spite of the efforts to save them. That was another thing she refused to talk about; but even so, the fact that they were all in disgrace together on Saturdays was still something that made them stick more than ever close to one another.

Shopping in Haimston, after all, was the weekend diversion for most families in the village, with sometimes a visit to the cinema thrown in for good measure; and once their mother had departed along with all the others who caught the midday bus, they felt very obviously left out of things. It was easier to put up with this feeling together, than separately, easier to persuade themselves they didn't look all that conspicuous. But that forlorn sort of feeling didn't last, of course—not once their father had said they must find something better to do than wander around like three lost sheep and Meg had decided what that something should be.

"We'll spend the time in Ballinford Woods," she announced. "There's always plenty to see and do there, this time of the year."

Meg was still their leader, even though she was so much in disgrace. And they had always done what Meg wanted when she spoke like that—ordering their moves, yet still with her voice giving out a note of excitement that enticed them to follow her as much as the words themselves commanded. Besides which, this was one occasion when they knew that Meg was perfectly right. The woods were blazing in their autumn red and russet and gold. There were brambles, and rowans, and hazelnuts there, all ripe and ready for picking. With miles of pathway to roam, too, they promised a freedom that they sensed would make up for their being outcasts. And so, every Saturday after that time, they set off for the woods—but always skirting the farm to begin with, so that they wouldn't have to pass Mrs. Torrie's house and perhaps see her on her way to the bus.

Mrs. Torrie was still in her mind, dancing there along with the other monster figure. She would do anything to avoid meeting either of them again, in the flesh!

"I won't go with you, otherwise," she insisted to Meg and Linda; and because she could find no way of explaining those feelings of revulsion and dread, they thought this was just another example of her contrary streak—the thing that made their mother say she had something "thrawn" in her nature. They argued with her. The back road into the woods was too muddy, they said. But still she persisted until they did agree to go that way; and it was the very fact of their agreement to it that led to the first of those things that did eventually matter. All three of them struck up an acquaintance with Blind Toby. But she herself became his friend.

Toby was nine, and he was the son of Mr. Gillan, the Earl's factor. He hadn't always been blind. That was due to an illness he'd had when he was a baby—before his mother died, they said. Now it was Mrs. Tait, a sort of nurse-housekeeper, who looked after him; but Toby had very little company apart from her, because his father worked long hours on the business of the estate. The house that went with Mr. Gillan's job, also, lay a good half-mile deep in the woods, which meant that hardly anyone used the path leading past the foot of its garden. And Toby was desperate for company. They found that out the very first time they saw him in the garden playing about with a big colored ball, kicking it into the air and then listening for the sound of it falling so that he could run to get it again.

He could do this quite easily, they noticed. There were no flowers in the garden, no bushes, nothing that could trip him up. The grass was cut very short, too, so that he could always run straight and quite fast to the ball. He left the ball where it lay, however, that first day he heard their voices, and came running straight to the fence instead, crying out as he ran,

"Speak to me! Speak to me, please!"

His hands came stretching through the fence, touching their clothes, feeling the baskets they were carrying for the bramble-picking. They were small hands, white and clean. Toby's skin was all white and clean—not like that of any other boy they knew. It was delicate, almost transparent, like flower petals. His eyes were gray, and big. There was a fixed stare to them; and sometimes when he was listening, he flapped his hand in front of them in a sort of fanning movement, as if this could somehow flap their blindness away.

"Who are you? What're your names? How old are you? Where are you going? What will you do with those baskets? May I touch your faces?"

Toby was full of questions. They told him about themselves, and gave him some of the brambles they had picked on the way to his house. They were big berries, black and ripe, with just the right touch of frost on them to make them sweet. Toby crammed them into his mouth, and the purple juice ran all over, staining his fingers and lips and white face till he looked like a little clown.

"Mrs. Tait'll be cross with you," Meg said, and tried to scrub the stains away with her hankie.

"I don't mind. She's always cross," Toby said, and went on asking questions.

Every time they met him he had questions, and it wasn't long before he knew even more about them than they said, because Mrs. Tait talked to everybody in the village and knew all the gossip. But Toby didn't mind them being in disgrace, and they didn't mind him knowing about it. They felt too sorry for Toby, really, to mind anything he said—except for Meg, of course, when he tried to ask anything about the Paddy woman.

And Toby wasn't stupid. He could tell as much from what he heard as other people could tell from what they saw, and he knew by the way Meg spoke then, that there was no use in persisting for an answer. But Toby had other questions that he did persistently ask—all sorts of odd questions they had never expected to hear.

"What color is the wind?" That was one of the things he wanted to know, and he wouldn't believe it when Meg and Linda said it was no color at all.

"It is a color. It is," he insisted. "*You* say which one, Jinty."

"It's the color of the way it makes you feel," she told him. "A warm wind is gold, and a cold one is gray."

"Don't be daft!" Linda exclaimed. "What's the use of saying things like that when he doesn't even know what color *is*?"

"I do, I do now." Toby contradicted. "Gold is warm, and gray is cold. How high is the sky, Jinty?"

"It's almost near enough to touch, in winter," she told him. "But in summer, the sky is forever."

Linda laughed at this, but Toby fanned his hand across his eyes and said eagerly, "I can see that! I can see how far away the sky is now."

Meg didn't say a thing about Linda laughing that day—not until they had gone on beyond Toby's garden and there was no danger of his hearing her. Then she really did speak her mind about it.

"There's a lot Toby hears that doesn't make sense to him," she said. "You can't expect it to do that—not with him being a blind boy that's never known anything in his life but being shut up in a bare garden. But if Jinty can help him to make his own kind of sense out of it, then you've no right to laugh at either of them. And you'd better not do it again."

Meg had changed in some way—and it wasn't just that she was accepting her punishment calmly, or that she was any less bouncy and cheerful than she had always been. There was also a sort of sureness about her, that hadn't been there before the night of the kirn—as if she knew so well where she was going now that there was no need for her to fly into rebellious rages the way she used to do. And there was the same kind of sureness in her voice when she spoke about Toby that day.

Linda could hear it too. Linda grumbled and protested that Meg had no right to order her around, but it still wasn't hard to see she was both aware of the sureness and curious about it. They all continued with gathering brambles. Linda kept on shooting curious glances at Meg; and every time this happened, something hovered in the air—something uneasy. But for the moment, at least, that was as far as it went. There was no open row between the two of them, nothing that might have put an end to the fascinating business of finding answers to the odd questions Toby asked; and she was glad of that. Toby was only a little kid, after all, and it would really have been a shame if she had been forced to disappoint him.

"Bring me flowers, Jinty," he begged her. "Please, will you? I want to see what flowers look like, and there's none in my garden."

Linda's mouth silently formed the word "see," but the look in Meg's eye stopped the sound of it.

"It's a bit late in the year for flowers, Toby." Cautiously, because she didn't want him to expect too much, she explained. But there were still Michaelmas daisies and dahlias and chrysanthemums to bring in single blooms so that she could let his fingers feel the shape while she tried to describe the colors in ways he could understand.

"Jaggedy-hot" for "red." That was easy. "A sunny day that's still cold." That was easy, too, for "yellow." But what could she say for "purple"?

"It's like a taste," she decided eventually. "You think it's going to be jaggedy-hot, like red; but when you do taste it, it slides away into something smoother, and really cold."

Toby laughed at this, and fanned his hand across his eyes as if to make himself see purple, stuck out his tongue as if he were tasting it. But once the frost had killed all the flowers in her own garden, and in the hedgerows as well, there was nothing she could do except to say she would bring more flowers in the spring.

"Snowdrops," she promised. "They're the first through the ground; small flowers, like little white bells dancing around."

"Do they ring like bells?" Toby asked; and she told him,

"Of course not, silly. Flowers don't make a noise.

You'll have to make the ringing sound yourself if you want to hear bells."

"You really do understand that kid, don't you?" Meg asked, and she felt the sort of embarrassed pleasure she always got from Meg's approval. But Linda immediately said,

"They're both crazy, that's why."

The uneasy something hovered in the air again— the feeling that you had to be careful with Linda. The lecture Meg had given about Toby wasn't forgotten, and Linda could be spiteful. But nothing came of the feeling then, either, because Meg's mind had already moved on to something else. Her head was to one side. She was listening for the guns of the shooting parties the Earl gave every winter, because that was the great diversion with them now—to mark the sound of the guns, then to find a path that would circle the line of fire, and so bring them to the excitement at the rear of the shoot where the beaters shouted and flailed their sticks to send the pheasants rocketing from cover.

Ahead of them the tall trees that had so recently flamed in bright colors stood as gaunt and dark as the pillars of some vast, burned-out cathedral. The path between them was broad and straight, but on either side of it were the narrow twisting tracks that could lead them safely to the position of the guns. They heard these at last, ahead and to their right, and chose a leftward path to begin the circling movement.

They had to walk in single file then, with Meg ahead, herself next, and Linda bringing up the rear. The track was thickly lined with a growth of elder and rowan, and as she plodded on with her eyes downward to the twisting line of brown earth between the thin, bare stems, she had her usual comfortable feeling that there was no need for her to plan against meeting the Earl at the shoot, the way she had planned against meeting Mrs. Torrie. The Earl was a great sportsman at everything from flying his private monoplane to riding point-to-point at Haimston Races, but he never attended his own shooting parties. He never shot at all, in fact, never so much as handled a gun. Everybody knew that; and so, when they were making towards the shoot, there always was this pleasant sense that the excitement ahead held no danger at all of meeting suddenly again with the monster still lurking in her imagination.

Vague sounds from ahead began to reach her—voices, and a thudding noise that she could not place. Were they at the shoot already? She looked up, and along the path; and in the same instant, Meg shouted,

"Get to the side! Jinty, Linda! Quickly! Into the side of the path!"

Automatically she reacted, squeezing hard back against the hedge of rowan and elder stems, but too surprised as yet to be frightened by the urgency in Meg's voice. Then she saw the source of the thudding noise—ahead of her and coming on at a fast walking pace, a party of riders on horses from the Earl's stables. And then she was afraid. The path was so narrow that the horses would have to pass within inches of her; and they were tall beasts, shiny-flanked hunters with long, slender legs—the kind that always frightened her with their nervous stamping when the Earl's grooms brought them to Archie Meikle to be shod.

"Stay still," Meg warned.

The horses began passing them in a smell of sweat and leather harshly overlying fainter scents—perfume, and the expensive clothes of the riders. Voices floated down to her, loud voices, laughing and talking in the incomprehensible drawl of southern England.

"The Master Race!" That was an explosive memory of Archie Meikle's ironic comment on the Earl's kind of guests bursting suddenly in her mind, making her even more afraid, because none of the riders was looking down. None of them was paying the least attention to the three forms pressed hard back against the hedging. And the horses' legs were so close, so dangerously close. They were long and muscular and iron-shod, and if she fell—if this swaying giddiness made her fall, as it must do at any moment—the hooves would trample right over her. . . .

6

She became aware of pain in either arm—
Meg on one side, Linda on the other, each of them
still with the grip that had seized her just as she sagged
forward. The horses had gone past, and with wonder
in her voice, Linda was saying,

"She's green! For God's sake, will you look at her!
I've *heard* of people going green with fright, but I
never thought it could actually happen!"

"I'm all right." Weakly she brushed at the hands and
tried to straighten, although she would dearly have
loved to lay her head against Meg and cry. "It's just—
They've always scared me at the smithy. It's the only
thing I don't like about the smithy—them coming to be
shod. And none of these people *cared.* They just didn't
bother if we got hurt."

"You didn't expect them to care, did you?" Linda
asked. "Village brats—that's all we are to them." She
sounded bitter, angry in a cold way that was the very

opposite to Archie's jovial jeering.

"Sit down, Jinty." Meg began pressing her down against the moss edging the path, and then looked up at Linda to ask,

"What's wrong with being a village brat? I like belonging to the village."

Linda jerked her head towards the vanished riders. "That's what's wrong with it. These people can kick people like us around. They've got money. They can do as they like."

"Then you'll have to do as Mam says, won't you?" Meg retorted. "Make something of yourself. Get a good job. Then you'll be away from the village and it won't matter to you."

"D'you think you're telling me anything I haven't thought out for myself? I've got a better brain than you any day, Meg Morrison. *And* I know how to use it."

She was crouched between them, and above her head they were facing one another like enemies. Meg looked taken aback by the fierce contempt in Linda's voice, and Linda—Did Linda realize how much she was showing of herself now? Nobody could ever have said she had a pretty face, of course. Lively, quick, interesting—there were all sorts of other ways to describe Linda's face. But not now. Not with all those lines of resentment on it; not with that bitter twist of spite on her lips.

"I'll tell you another thing," Linda said. "You'll never

get me spoiling the field for myself with anything so stupid as sneaking out to the kirn."

"No," Meg answered. "You never did believe in taking chances."

"That's right." Linda agreed. "But just you wait till I'm onto a sure thing!"

They stared in silence at one another, then Meg bent down to ask,

"How're you now, Jinty? Okay?"

"Och, yes, I'm fine." She started to rise, glancing along the path as she did so, and saw a last, lone horseman coming around the bend ahead. The branches of elder stretching across the path at that point made an arch that framed him. A shaft of sunlight striking through the ragged remains of their yellow leaves, briefly illumined first the horse and then its rider as well; but it didn't need this to tell her who he was.

"The Earl!" The dread following hard on her recognition brought a catch into her voice as she half spoke, half whispered the words. Meg and Linda followed her glance, and then crowded beside her, against the undergrowth, backing hard into it to leave room for him to pass. The horse came on—a big chestnut-colored beast, stepping slower than the other ones had done, as if it had been ridden harder than they. The tall figure swaying in the saddle stared straight ahead, seeming no more aware of them than if they had been part of the undergrowth itself. She held her breath, waiting for the horse to pass, but at the last second

73

before it drew level with them, its head jerked up in response to a pull on the reins. It halted, and there he was staring down at them, eyes palely glinting, robber-chief face seeming bigger and redder than ever—the monster-face that had grinned above the dying Paddy woman. . . .

"The Morrison girls, eh?" He was speaking to them now, and when they answered with nods, he went on, "And d'you know there's shooting going on in these woods?"

It was to Meg he said this, his eyes fastening on her as the eldest of the group; and boldly she told him,

"Yes, of course we know."

"And have you the sense to keep behind the guns?"

"That's what we were doing," Meg said. "We were just working our way up to the rear of the shoot when the horses came past."

He was even closer to them than the other riders had been. And he looked huge. He was looming over her, the breadth, the height of him, dark against the sunlit leaves; a heavy tower of dread looming, with the smell of tweed and leather and horse sweat and man sweat all mixed and thick in her nostrils. . . .

"That child—your young sister—is she ill?"

The question and the look that came with it made her remember the priest. *"Is that child always so white?"* But Linda had said she'd gone green with fright over the horses; and so what color was she now? She felt a sudden impulse to hysterical laughter, and it was the effort of will needed to control this that steadied her. But she still couldn't answer, and it was Meg who said,

"She'll be all right in a minute. It was just the horses passing. She was scared of them."

"H'mmm. She looks scared of me now." His eyes came back to Meg. "But you're not. Not by a long chalk, it seems."

Meg gave a little laugh at this; and then—not boasting, but just being quite truthfully Meg—she said, "I'm not scared of anyone."

The Earl didn't laugh. Instead, he seemed startled. His eyes roamed Meg's face, as if searching it for something he knew ought to be there. Then he nodded, and like a man speaking to himself, he said,

"Yes—but that's what I should have expected, of course. Courage. The same kind."

They always said that the Earl knew everything about everybody in the village; but there was still something odd about all this, something that made it unrelated to any obvious meaning. And while Meg was staring as if she had also thought like this, he asked her,

"Being punished for sneaking out to the kirn, aren't you?"

"Yes, I am." Meg sounded quite cool, but there was still a note of defiance in her voice, and this time the Earl did laugh before he told her,

"Well, it was a childish thing to do, you know, to disobey your mother's ruling."

"I'll be fifteen in February," Meg said. "That's old

enough to dance with grown people."

The Earl gave her another long look. "It is now," he told her. "You were a child when you defied your mother, but it made you a woman grown to try to save a life by owning up to what you'd done."

Meg didn't answer, but she flushed, the quick bright flush that so easily colored her white skin; and for some reason, this made the Earl look all the harder at her. He started to say something, then changed his mind, and told them all instead,

"All right then, on you go. But remember what I said about keeping behind the guns. I don't want all my gamekeepers complaining about kids spoiling the shoot."

They stood looking after him as he flicked the reins and moved off, and as soon as he seemed to be out of earshot, Linda swung round to challenge Meg,

"What was all that about? What did he mean—'the same kind'? The same as what?"

"I don't know," Meg protested. "Unless—Maybe it was just that I reminded him of somebody."

"Of course, you ninny! But who? Who? He said *That's what I should have expected.* Why should he expect you to look like this somebody?"

"It could have been Dad," Meg offered. "Or Mam. He knows them both well enough."

Linda stared at her. "You're dumb," she said witheringly. "You really are dumb. You don't even look like Mam, the way Jinty and I do, and the only way you take after Dad is being big, like him. It was what you said to the Earl—*'I'm not scared of anyone.'* And the way you said it, with that 'Let the whole world come at me' air of yours. And you're very much mistaken if you think it's from Dad you get that air. Or from Mam."

"All right. So that was it." Meg shrugged, clearly not wanting another row. "But you don't need to keep on about it, the way you're doing."

"Maybe not. But there's still a mystery, if you ask me."

Linda's eyes were narrowed with curiosity as she spoke, and it was this that stung Meg, at last, into retaliation.

"I don't ask you!" she shouted. "And stop looking at me like that, Linda Morrison, with your eyes all piggy and curious!"

With a quick, plunging movement, she turned to hurry along the path, then stopped abruptly, as if remembering something. Looking back, she called,

"Come on, Jinty. I'd better take you home."

"Yes, poor wee soul," Linda said. The tone was more than enough to warn her it was her own turn to be teased, and as she moved closer to Meg she got ready to defend herself. "The Earl was right," Linda called after her. "You *are* scared of him."

"No, I'm not," she threw back over her shoulder—quickly, because Linda was the last person she could tell of that terrible vision on the night of the kirn, and all the peculiar feelings it had left with her. Linda was too sensible to have monsters in her mind. "At least, it's just sometimes I am, like—you know—when I think of the way people call him 'the bad old Earl.'"

To her relief then, Meg began to take her part. "I'm not surprised at that," she said. "It made him seem like a sort of bogeyman to me, too, when I was little."

Linda started towards them then, her face changing as if she had suddenly decided to stop teasing. "I can remember that," she said. "You used to take my hand and tell me to run past the smithy when we saw him talking there to Archie Meikle."

Meg laughed at this, but it was friendly laughter; and after it, the argument just seemed to melt away. Linda mimicked the Earl's voice, catching the note of it exactly, the way she always did when she imitated anyone. They all laughed then, and Linda said,

"Jinty's got her proper color back."

"Yes, I'm fine now," she agreed. And because she really did feel all right again, they decided there was no need for her to go home after all. They went on to the shoot instead, just as they had meant to do; but even although they did eventually enjoy themselves there, it still seemed to her that it wasn't the same for them as it had been on past occasions. Something seemed to have gone out of the way they enjoyed it, some of the feeling of closeness they had always had before then; and at first she thought this was because Meg and Linda had so recently argued. But as the time of their punishment went on towards its end, she still had this feeling of something missing, and at last she pinned down the real reason for the loss.

It wasn't because they had become any less loyal to one another than they had always been; nor was it because they expected less from their expeditions to the woods. It was something that had been happening to Meg and Linda in the course of these expeditions; some basic difference in their natures that had begun to show itself. And now it was plain enough to tell her that things could never be the same again, for any of them. They had come to the end of their time as a close-knit family group; and the way Meg and Linda were behaving showed that they, too, realized this.

Each Saturday after that, she noticed, they were becoming more guarded with one another; as if each were taking the other's measure for the time they would be able to go their separate ways. And the more she realized this, the keener her sense of loss became. The end of the ban on shopping trips to Haimston was no longer attractive then—besides which, she had yet another reason for wanting things to go on as they had been doing. Toby. There were only certain times of day when Toby was allowed into his garden, and she was determined not to desert him so that she could join the others on that Saturday bus at midday.

"I'm not going," she had to say eventually when the time came to put this to the test. "I can't go. I promised Toby I'd see him just the same as on the other Saturdays."

79

They were all staring at her, her father and mother, too, all of them except her father stopping in the middle of getting ready to go out to the bus. Meg had a sort of guilty look. Her mother frowned, as if trying to place something in her mind, and then asked,

"Toby? That's Toby Gillan, the factor's son, isn't it? The blind child."

"We used to see him every Saturday when we went to the woods," Meg said quickly. "Jinty got fond of him—we all did. But the way Jinty talks to him, she can make him see things."

"Crazy talk," Linda added. "Colors like tastes, and all that."

Nobody said anything for a moment. She stood there, feeling herself trapped in the oddity Linda's words had ascribed to her, and sorry for herself because of this. Then her mother asked,

"*Is* that how you talk to him?"

She nodded, not wanting to trust speech in case they heard her self-pity in it.

"And you enjoy that?"

"He does. Toby does." She felt herself forced to hedge, for fear the rest of them really would think she was crazy, like Linda did. She saw her father and mother exchange looks; then her mother said gently,

"All right, then. But just don't put too much store on being friendly with Toby. He's—Well, for one thing he's a lot younger than you."

There had been something in that look between her

parents. She didn't understand it. She didn't understand, either, why her mother had spoken like that, in such a gentle voice; and it all gave her the feeling that she ought to try to explain herself.

"I took him flowers, you see. He liked that. He liked me to describe the colors to him. But there won't be any more until the spring comes. And I can't just leave him with nobody to talk to till then, can I?"

"I said it was all right for you to go." Her mother's voice got a bit sharper with this, but her father gave another of those looks, and said,

"How about this for him, then, until you can get more flowers?"

He held up finger and thumb as he spoke, and showed her one of the wood carvings he had done that winter—a tiny figure of a squirrel, bushy tail up-curled, a nut held between its front paws. She looked at it, longing to take it, but not quite sure of what he had meant. Her hand came half up to it before she asked,

"To keep?"

"Why not? Goodness knows I've plenty to give you a different one every week, if you want. Here!"

She was embarrassed by the curiosity in their eyes as she caught it, and backed away with it in her hand. The thought of that went with her along the lane while she ran towards Toby's house; but once she was there, it didn't matter any more—not when she saw how much Toby liked the squirrel.

"You can keep it," she told him. "And I'll get you other things. My Dad carves them and he says you can have more."

The cold weather had made Toby's face whiter than ever. The color of the carving—a reddish-brown that had hardly shown against her father's hand—looked very dark when he held it to his cheek; but she was too busy explaining the way a squirrel moved and the sound it made, to do more than just notice this in passing. Then there was the owl she brought the following Saturday. It was hard for Toby to understand how an owl could see in the dark, when "dark" and "blind" meant the same to him. That took a lot more explaining, but the next week was a rabbit, which gave her no problems at all; and it was then that she realized how terribly frail he really was.

"You'd better go in," she told him when he started coughing in the middle of one of his questions. "I think you might be ill if you don't."

Toby didn't want to go in, but she insisted, and the next week she wasn't surprised to see the doctor's car standing in the driveway of the house. After that, although she went faithfully every Saturday, she didn't see much of Toby. Sometimes the doctor's car was waiting in the drive, and there was no sign of Toby at all. Sometimes she saw him at the far end of the garden with a tall, gray-haired man, both of them walking slowly and stopping every now and then to let Toby cough. The tall man was Mr. Gillan; and so, she thought, Toby did at least have his father for company.

On another two occasions, however, she was not so pleased to see the Earl's Rolls-Royce standing in the driveway.

It seemed quite shameful to her, in fact, that the Earl should come to take up Mr. Gillan's time with business when Toby needed him enough to make him stay home from the estate office on Saturdays; and going back towards the smithy, which was where she had taken to spending the remainder of these Saturdays, she felt indignant about it.

"Toby's ill," she said to Archie Meikle, after the second time she had seen the Rolls. "You know—Blind Toby."

"Aye, I do know," Archie told her. "The doctor's been at him."

"The Earl's been there, too," she said. "Twice. I saw his car in the drive."

"And?" Archie gave a backhanded swipe at the sweat on his face as he waited for her to go on.

"Well, it's mean to Toby, isn't it?" she asked. "He's only little, after all, and if he's sick enough to need his Dad at home, it *is* mean of the Earl to take up Mr. Gillan's time with business."

"Is that a fact?" Archie exclaimed; but that was only his way of saying "Well, I never," or something else to show he was surprised. She nodded, feeling she had made her point, and then was taken aback to hear him say sternly,

"You've got a lot to learn, miss, if that's the way your mind's working!"

She backed away then, both bewildered and hurt at the way Archie had turned on her, and told herself afterwards that it was only because he was so thick with the Earl that he had put her down like that. The carved animals began to accumulate in her pockets, meanwhile, but that wasn't anything to bother about, she decided. Toby had enough of these to be going on with until he was allowed to go out again by himself, and he wouldn't be so keen on them by that time anyway, because then she would be able to bring the snowdrops she had promised. They were all out in the gardens by the end of February, and that meant there would be masses of them in the woods.

She made up her mind to pick some before she went up on the following Saturday, just in case he was better by then. On Friday of that week she went to school thinking that she would go straight from there to the woods to get a really big bunch of them; and it was on that Friday she heard that Toby was dead.

7

It was from Miss Carson she heard the news. Miss Carson spoke to the whole class, just before school broke up for the day.

"Please all listen quietly now. I have an announcement to make. There will be no school on Monday afternoon—"

A buzz of excitement going around the class, herself sharing in it, plans already leaping into her head. And then, Miss Carson's voice raised over the buzz,

"—owing to the death of Mr. Gillan's son, Toby. The funeral will be at three P.M. on Monday; and, as a mark of respect from Ballinford Estate, the Earl has requested that no work should be done in the village on that afternoon. As Chairman of the School Board, also, he has decided that the same observance will apply to all classes in the school; and you will therefore dismiss for the day at the time of the dinner bell on Monday."

There was nothing more to it than that—a bald statement, like a notice in the newspaper. Nothing about Toby being only nine, or never having had anyone but a crosspatch like Mrs. Tait to look after him. The school bell rang, and its clangor shouted at her, *"Or fanning his eyes, or sticking out his tongue to taste purple, or calling 'Speak to me! Speak to me!'"*

It didn't seem real—not any of it; the cool voice of Miss Carson, any more than the loud one of the bell. Neither of them gave her mind anything to take hold of, and feel that the news about Toby was really true.

At home, they expected her to cry. That was what the waiting look on their faces said, as they all sat around the supper table. Her mother had made a cake, with icing on it. Her mother had a sweet tooth, and so had she herself; and that was her mother's way of showing sympathy. But what do you do when Toby dies and someone says kindly, *"I'm sure you could do with another slice, Jinty."* She ate the cake, and the icing was like glue in her mouth, sticking there until she could hardly move her jaws and the cake was a soggy, choking mess.

Why didn't she cry? A month before that, they'd had trouble with one of the chinchilla rabbits her father bred for their fur—a doe that had persisted in overlying her young; and because she had not been able to bear the thought of the whole litter dying like that, she had persuaded her father to let her try to bring up the only two of it that were left. Then she *had* cried to find them

86

one morning, lying cold and stark in the shoe box she had so carefully lined with wool for them. Kneeling in front of the kitchen fire, not caring that she looked ridiculous with her face right down beside the box on the hearth rug and her backside sticking up in the air, she had cried—howled, in fact—with grief over the two dead rabbits. Why didn't she cry like that now? Why couldn't she cry like that for Toby?

"They're only a couple of young rabbits. Do the sensible thing with them, girl. Bury them."

They would do the sensible thing with Toby. At three o'clock on Monday afternoon. He was only a small blind boy, and they would bury him.

"How's the cake?" her mother asked. "Enjoying it, are you, dearie?"

"It's great." Through the sweet, gluey mess she mumbled the lying words, and with a sense of appalled wonder saw how completely her mother accepted them—her father as well, both of them beaming approval at her, sure that the stratagem of the cake had worked.

All through that weekend, too, and at school on Monday morning, she had the oddest feeling that there was someone else—some stranger—moving her limbs, and using her voice to speak; and the truly weirdest part of all this was that she seemed to know ahead of time just what this stranger would do or say with her body and her voice. Like it was when the school dinner bell rang on Monday and she knew then that, instead of rushing home as she usually did, the stranger was going to use her body to walk up to the woods where the snowdrops grew thickest.

She was there, without knowing how long it had taken to reach the place, without seeing anything on the way, and the snowdrops were all around her in waves of white that shivered and turned tinges of green to the winds that moved them. It was the first time she had been alone in that cool and green-tinged whiteness of February. Always before, there had been Meg and Linda wandering with her and stooping to pick great bunches of the snowdrops. And it was Meg who had taught her how to pick, sliding her fingers gently down the stem of each flower to explore its maximum length, and then breaking it cleanly away from its shield of leaves.

The stranger who was managing her fingers did the same now, wisely selecting the flowers that seemed to have the longest stems, skillfully nipping them off without damage to the plant itself, neatly bundling the flowers within a circle of their own spiky greenery. The stranger dug into her pockets, knowing that they held scraps of wool put there in preparation for tying up the bundles. The stranger was pleased at the foresight and at the choice of wool for the job, knowing also that elastic bands or twine would have cut into the fragile stems of the flowers. The hands came out clutching the small carved figures of a deer and a badger among the bits of wool, and all this had to be carefully separated before the first bunches of snowdrops could be tied.

Moving cautiously—it was wicked to trample flowers, her father said—she went on allowing the hands to pick. Now that she was there, there seemed no point in not doing that; and it was only when her arms were full, with one bunch piled on another, that the stranger stopped her from bending, and edging forward through the snowdrop sea. The same decision sent her back the way she had come, walking slowly so as not to damage the flowers, out of the woods by the back road that took her passing by Toby's house—as she must have passed it on the way there, she realized. But she—or the stranger inside her, rather—hadn't been aware of it then. And now she was. She—Jinty—saw that the blinds were drawn. The house was dead. Toby was dead. And so why had she picked the snowdrops? What could she do with them?

She walked faster, no longer careful of the flowers. She was clutching them hard, and her grip brought a fresh, scentless smell rising from them. The mud of the back road into the woods met the surfaced road running to the village, and she walked along this with her nostrils full of the bruised-flower smell. Ahead of her was the church; and outside the church, the road was edged with a long line of cars and pony-traps. The gate to the churchyard was open, and from beyond the gate came a sort of murmuring—voices, and movements, in a subdued mingling of sounds.

She stopped. There was no stranger inside her now. She was simply Jinty stopping by the churchyard gate, knowing that Toby's funeral was in progress, and with her arms full of flowers—foolishly so, when she didn't even know why she had picked them. There was a great knot of people around one point in the churchyard— all men. Women didn't go to funerals, her mother said. Not in Scotland, anyway. It wasn't seemly for women to go to funerals. They were the ones who stayed at home with the blinds drawn.

She could see Mr. Gillan among the men. He was all gray. A tall gray man in a gray suit with a black arm-band around its left sleeve; gray hair, a gray face. Archie Meikle was there, in his dark, Sunday-go-to-meeting suit. So was her father. All the men in the village were there, in fact, all in their Sunday-go-to-meetings. The Earl was there too, but he wore his usual blue-brown tweeds, with a black armband around the sleeve of his jacket. He was standing beside Mr. Gillan, and as she watched, she saw him put an arm around Mr. Gillan's shoulders.

There was a little movement among the men, and out of this came the fluttering black of Mr. Elphinston's clerical robe. Mr. Elphinston's voice sounded. It was an unusually quiet voice for him, and she thought the low, droning noise it made must be a prayer. She froze there, not daring to move until this was finished; and it was in this frozen moment that the Earl turned his head and saw her standing with her armful of flowers, at the gate.

Mr. Elphinston's voice stopped. Mr. Gillan and the Earl both bent to pick up something—the cords at the head of Toby's coffin, she realized. The coffin was small, and white. Archie Meikle and Mr. Nelson, the farm manager, held the cords at the foot of it. The four men straightened, lifting the small white box clear of the ground. They swung it sideways, and then let the cords slip gently through their hands as they lowered it downwards. The lowering movement stopped. The four men allowed the cords to drop from their hands, and then the Earl turned and beckoned her towards himself.

Automatically, she obeyed the beckoning gesture, but embarrassment at all the faces now watching her, kept her steps slow. She halted in front of the Earl, looking up at him, wondering why she had been summoned. He didn't speak—just took her by the shoulders and turned her to face the grave. She looked down into it—a brown hole with crumbling edges, the coffin gleaming white at the foot of it; and then she understood. Her arms began to unclench their tight hold. She leaned forward, letting them open wider, releasing the bunches of snowdrops from them.

"Do they ring like bells?"

Toby would have to make the ringing sound himself. The snowdrops cascaded downwards, and landed in a spreading heap of white and green on the whiteness below. A number of the men standing around took out handkerchiefs and began blowing their noses; loudly, and fussing about it, as if it had suddenly become important to do this properly. Nobody looked at Mr. Gillan, but it wouldn't have made any difference if they had. Mr. Gillan had his head bent and his handkerchief covering nearly the whole of his face. The Earl touched her shoulder and she glanced up at him again.

There was a tired, drawn look to his face. Its features seemed more than ever craggy, but there were folds and wrinkles among them that she had never noticed there before, and some of the high color had drained from them. It wasn't the monster-face of her imagination any more, in fact. It was just an old man's face, as bleak and grieving as any of the others there. The Earl nodded down at her—partly, it seemed to her, in approval, and partly in dismissal; and she turned to walk away from him with all sorts of rapid adjustments going on in her mind.

The times she had seen the Rolls-Royce parked in the driveway when Toby was ill—perhaps the Earl hadn't been calling on business then, after all. Perhaps he had been there to comfort Mr. Gillan, like he had comforted him with that arm around his shoulder. And if that was so, wouldn't it explain what Archie Meikle had told her? *"If that's the way you're thinking, miss, you've still got a lot to learn."*

Then there was the beckoning gesture the Earl had made when he had seen her at the gate. There would be no puzzle about that, would there, if the reason for his visits had also been to see Toby himself? Toby hadn't had anything to look forward to, after all, except the snowdrops; and what with that, and him being such a talker, he was bound to have told any visitor about her promise to bring them.

Something stirred in her mind. The Ballinford doom—and Tom Meikle saying of the Earl, "*He dotes on his son.*" Toby had been an only son. Lord Garvald was an only son. Had that made a sort of bond between the Earl and Mr. Gillan? And if that was so, what had the Earl been thinking of when he stood there at Toby's funeral? Of the doom on his own son? Wondering, perhaps, how and when Lord Garvald would die?

"Jinty!" She heard her father's voice behind her, and turned, waiting for him. He closed with her in long strides, and after they had walked on together a few steps, he said quietly,

"Feeling all right, are you?"

He was inviting her to talk about Toby, she realized; but she didn't want to do that. Later, perhaps, she might feel that way, but not now; not until she had got out of the habit of inventing ways to tell Toby about colors. Once she had done that she would be able to stop thinking about him fanning his hand across his eyes, and perhaps the ache she would feel then would be no worse than what was left of the one for the rabbits in the shoe box.

"Yes, of course," she answered. "I'm fine."

Her father didn't say anything to this, just looked doubtfully at her; and as much to divert attention from herself as for any other reason, she went on,

"I was thinking, that's all. Back there, just now, the Earl looked different from the way I always thought he was."

Her father gave a sort of half laugh, and said, "You're learning."

"Learning what?"

"That nicknames like 'the bad old Earl' spring from hearsay; and hearsay is poor ground for forming a true judgment on anyone."

Something in his tone warned her then to keep quiet, and after they had walked on a bit farther, he said,

"When the War was finished and I came out of the army, all I knew about was soldiering. I was just a young man, too, but I had—Well, I had responsibilities; your mother, and Meg, and Linda. That made me desperate to get work. But I had no training for anything, and the unemployment in the land was terrible. That was when the Earl gave me the job I have now. I'd have finished up in the gutter selling matches, otherwise."

Like the men she'd seen in Haimston, she thought; ragged, dirty men, with the faces of beaten creatures, standing in the gutter of Haimston High Street with trays of matches, and bootlaces, and tape, slung around their necks. And hanging from the trays, the notices that read, *Unemployed ex-soldier. Wife and children to support. Please help.*

An echo of her mother's voice came into her mind— the wintertime voice that always had a high note of worry in it because Meg and Linda had needed their

Academy uniforms replaced for the start of the new school year; and if the money wouldn't stretch to cover everything else, after that big expense, the groceries might have to be left owing. The echoing voice made her wonder if they were really so much better off than the families of the match-tray men, and with a sudden feeling of sympathy for her mother, she said impatiently,

"The Earl's rich. And he doesn't pay *you* much of a wage."

Her father sighed. "Look," he told her, "I don't have to be reminded that the Earl spends a dam' sight more on one of his horses in a week than he does on my wage. But I'm paid the rate for the job; and it was only because he was told of the fix I was in that he gave it to me in the first place. *That's* my point."

They walked on in silence after that, until finally her father said, "But he's still not an easy man to understand, Jinty; I grant you that. What's more, the longer you know him, the more you'll realize how many sides there are to his character."

"Such as?" she asked. But her father was not to be drawn any further on this—not then, or later; and it was not until Toby had been dead for nearly three months that she had cause to remember that last remark about the Earl, and to realize something of why her father had made it.

8

The summer term at school was halfway over by that time. All the gardens in the village were packed brightly with the flowers she would never be able to make Toby see now, but the small marker stone Mr. Gillan had put up in the churchyard still looked so new that it was hard not to notice it when she had to walk past it into church on Sunday mornings. The swallows had come back to the village by then also, swooping and swiftly darting over the rooftops of all the cottages, nesting under all the eaves; and it was the return of the swallows that lay at the beginning of her next experience of the Earl.

A pair of them nested inside the school that term, flying in through a window that had been left open at the weekend, and it was she who was first to see them at work on the nest. That was on the Monday morning, when she had to be early in school because it was her turn to be class monitor in Miss Carson's room; and the moment she became aware of the birds and of the cup-shape of mud forming against one of the ceiling beams, she forgot entirely about filling inkwells and all the other monitor jobs.

She stood quite still, watching their flight from window to beam and back to the window again. They were so swift, so handsome with their dark-blue backs and white breasts. That was something she would never have been able to describe to Toby—those two living arrows of midnight-blue and snow-white. And how skillfully they worked at the nest! With wonder she observed the way they clung to the beam, heads twisting around to daub each beakful of mud onto its place in the layers building up to the cup-shape. She was still not too entranced by this, however, to realize whom she could see passing the window eventually, and to be there at the door to meet Miss Carson with the story of what had happened over the weekend.

"And if we all keep quiet, miss," she finished, breathlessly, because she had talked so fast, "they'll go on with the nest and we'll be able to see it all, the young birds getting fed, and everything."

"Now, Janet," Miss Carson said, and immediately she felt her own face going slack with disappointment. It was going to be the same all over again. Lectures, lectures, and no illusions. "You're forgetting your exam," Miss Carson went on. "My classes have fifteen of you who'll have to sit the Qualifying this month."

That was true. And the Qualifying Exam was important. It was only by passing the Quali that you could get into the Academy. Miss Carson was waiting for her to admit this, but the disappointment choking in her throat would not allow her to do so in words. She nodded, instead. Miss Carson nodded too, and told her,

"Some things can be hard, Janet, but—"

They stared at one another—or at least Miss Carson stared, as if trying to read her thoughts, and she could not break away from the look. Then, abruptly, Miss Carson said,

"That blind child—your friend, Toby. I wish I'd known about him. I might have been able to do something. Teach him, perhaps."

She was embarrassed. It was like her mother's cake all over again—a sticky-sweet offering to take away the taste of death. It wasn't fair, either, to remind her like that, now it was all over. And besides, what could Miss Carson have taught Toby?

"Toby had illusions. But he needed them. He didn't have anything else."

She hadn't meant to say that aloud. It just came out, without her realizing at first that she had spoken it, instead of thinking it. Miss Carson gave her another long look, and went a little pink—just a faint flush creeping over the paleness of her face. After what seemed a long pause, then, she said—again abruptly,

"Very well, Janet, you've made your point. Now it's up to you and the rest of your class to prove it. Just so long as none of you takes advantage, that's all."

But none of them did take advantage, of course—not even the ones who were too young as yet to be making their run-up to the Quali; and right from the time Miss Carson gathered them all outside the classroom that morning to explain about the nest, they kept to the terms she made. So long as the work didn't suffer, she told them, they could watch the swallows any time they liked. They were to keep their voices low, not to fidget, and all their movements were to be made very slowly and cautiously. Nor was that so difficult as it sounded, because they were all so interested in the swallows that none of them wanted to do anything that might scare them. And there was no loud talking from Miss Carson herself, either; no lectures, no rapping of her pointer on the blackboard. There was an odd and yet very soothing sense of peace, in fact, in Miss Carson's room that term.

The swallows finished building their nest. The female bird began brooding on her eggs, with the male foraging food and flying in with it to her. The hatching of the eggs brought orange-colored throats poking from the nest, with a constant cheeping from the young ones and the parent birds perpetually swooping in to push food down their beaks. Then, in no time at all, it seemed, there were five fledglings clinging with sharp claws to the ceiling beam, and a wild fluttering and chirping as they made their first flight from it.

They watched it all, from start to finish. Miss Carson also watched, her neat dark head tilted back, brown-button eyes shining with interest. When their attention was not actually on the birds, she moved among their desks correcting work, always walking quietly so as not

99

to disturb the swallows, with only a finger coming down on a book here, a whispered word of advice sounding there. Miss Carson was quite changed, in fact, from the stern sergeant-major figure she had been before, to someone strangely gentle. It was amazing too, how helpful those whispers of advice could be. In spite of the swallow-silence and the time spent in staring upwards, they all had the feeling of learning faster than they ever had before; and it wasn't long before Mr. Hargreave, the Headmaster, began wondering at the improvement in their work.

Mr. Hargreave taught the Advanced Division—the ones who had failed the Quali and were really doing no more than marking time under his eye until they could leave school at fourteen. But it was Mr. Hargreave also, who held special classes for each year's new batch of Quali entrants, and that meant they had to spend several afternoons a week in his classroom. They grudged that. All of them grudged any time spent away from their swallow family; and they were annoyed too, about the way the big louts of the Advanced Division teased them over this—or did, at least, until Mr. Hargreave put a stop to it.

Mr. Hargreave knew about the swallows, of course, but he still hadn't realized how Miss Carson had changed since she began to watch them; and it was only when he kept on being so pleased with the work they did in her class that some of them were bold enough to tell him about this. Mr. Hargreave looked surprised at first, then interested; and finally, speaking more to himself than to them, he said,

"So our Miss Carson has at last discovered her human side, has she? Well, well. I think I could name some-one who'd like to know about that!"

He glanced around them, smiling as if he had some private sort of joke. Mr. Hargreave was like that. He had black hair and green eyes that made him look too young for a Headmaster, and he very often seemed to be privately smiling. There were times, too, when he didn't behave at all like a Headmaster; and what he did then was to sit down at the piano that was kept in his room for school music lessons. He struck a chord or two on this, and told them,

"There's a scrap of song I know that seems to suit the occasion."

The chords became a tum-ti-tum sort of tune, and as he rattled this out, Mr. Hargreave sang,

> "Birds in their little nests agree,
> Chirruping harmoniously
> They get along quite peaceably,
> Why, oh why can't we?"

They couldn't see the point of that, nor did they understand why Mr. Hargreave burst suddenly into laughter at the end of the verse. But once the exam was safely past, they did; because it was then that rumor ran wildfire around the village with news of a supposed engagement between Miss Carson and Tom Meikle. And on Monday morning of the week after the exam, Miss Carson herself confirmed the rumor by coming into school with a diamond ring on her engagement finger.

Mr. Hargreave began collecting money to give her a present when she left the school. She meant to do so, it seemed, at the end of that term, and she was to be married to Tom on the day following. There was enough in the collection to buy her a tea set—a very handsome one from a high-class shop in Edinburgh. But Mr. Hargreave had something up his sleeve apart from that; something the Earl wanted to do, and which was to be kept as a last-minute secret.

"And the Earl's the Chairman of the School Board, you know," Mr. Hargreave said; "which means we'll have to do as he says." But the smile was there in his green eyes as he spoke, that same sort of private smile he had given before he sang the silly verse. It was after school, and everyone had gone except themselves—the Quali pupils, and the younger ones in Miss Carson's room. Mr. Hargreave had arranged that, and it seemed he had arranged for the Earl to be there, too, because the next minute the Rolls was outside the school and the Earl was coming into the classroom to stand in front of them.

"Now then," he started, and his voice as well as his presence was so overpowering in that small space that she was glad the swallows had already flown the nest. "Mr. Hargreave tells me you all know a song—quite a famous one, it seems—called 'The Harmonious Black-smith.' Right? Well, Tom Meikle is by way of being a friend of mine, and so we're going to have a bit of a joke with that. Soon as the presentation is made to Miss Carson, you'll start singing the song—*That's George that I hear/ He swings the big hammer/ The clang and the clamor/*—and so on. Right? But instead of 'George,' you'll sing *'That's Tom that I hear.'* Meanwhile, all the chaps in the village will have gathered at the smithy. The moment you start singing, I'll give a signal from the window of the school hall and all the fellows at the smithy will start beating hell out of every bit of iron they can find there. They'll make a clang and a clangor all right! But young Tom won't suspect a thing until they start, and that'll be *his* baptism in the fire of mar-riage. Right?"

He was grinning now, a great broad grin that stretched right across his face, splitting the craggy red-ness of it wide open. It was impossible not to grin back at him; impossible not to join in with the great shout of everyone else repeating, *"Right!"*

Mr. Hargreave started talking, filling in all the details of what was to happen. The Earl listened along with the rest of them, the grin still on his face, and it was while she was watching him then that she remembered how her father had talked of him, on that day of Toby's funeral.

"The longer you know him the more you'll realize how many sides there are to his character."

It was the snowdrops and the bleakness of his face at

103

the graveside that had taught her there was more to him than the bogeyman she had feared when she was small, or the monster her imagination had created from that on the night of the kirn. But now, it seemed, there was more to know, much more, even, than she had guessed from the odd friendship between him and Archie Meikle. There was also this vast, grinning merriment at the joke he had thought up to play on Tom Meikle, and that made him even harder to understand. But there was still one thing at least that she was sure of now. She wasn't scared of him any more— or not much, anyway, and not in the same way as she used to be.

"Are you going to tell them the rest of it?" That was him speaking again, looking at Mr. Hargreave, keeping his voice low and glancing back at them as he added, "About Miss Carson and the smithy?"

"No," Mr. Hargreave decided. "I think that's Archie Meikle's business."

The Earl nodded. "You're right. Archie should be the one to explain that."

Explain what? The puzzle of the Earl's final words nagged at her mind every day of the week between then and Prize Day; and all through the prize-giving ceremony itself, it was still there at the back of her thoughts. But that Prize Day, of course, was so different to all the others she had known that this was just one more thing to add to the peculiar feelings it gave her.

For a start, there was hardly a man in the school hall, apart from Mr. Hargreave and the Earl, and it was unusual not to see a few fathers who had taken time off from work to be there. It was strange, also, to realize that those men who might have been there were among the ones gathered at the smithy; and it was the very fact of everyone knowing this that seemed to be creating a tense atmosphere in the hall.

Then there was the once-in-a-lifetime thrill of seeing Mr. Hargreave stand up to read the list of those who had passed the Qualifying; of hearing her own name called out, and of knowing then that, next year, she would be at the Academy. It was a pity, she thought, that her father was not there to hear it as well as her mother; and the thought made her realize the source of another and different sort of tension in her mind.

Her mother hadn't approved of Miss Carson's engagement to Tom Meikle. "A waste," she had called it. Miss Carson was just throwing away a good career; and rather than countenance that, she had declared, she would not go to the prize-giving at all. But she had relented, of course. The thought of hearing *"Janet Beatrice Morrison"* called out among the list of passes, had been responsible for that. Another of her girls—the third of them—to succeed in getting a higher education! Not for the world would her mother have missed that announcement. But that was all over now. There was nothing left to do except to present Miss Carson with the tea set. And what if that should bring the disapproval so obviously back to her mother's face?

From her place on the front benches along with the rest of Miss Carson's pupils, she searched anxiously for a sight of her mother, but the crowded appearance of the hall defeated her purpose. Uneasily she faced forward again to the low platform where the Earl sat with Mr. Hargreave on his right hand, Miss Carson, and Miss Baxter, the infants' teacher, on his left. Miss Carson was wearing a coral-pink dress, and maybe it was because the color suited her so much better than the brown of her school overall, but she looked younger than she usually did. She was wearing lipstick, too—something she had never done before, in school; and the coral-colored lips were an exact match for the shade of her dress.

Mr. Hargreave stood up to make his presentation speech. It was a very short one, but there was a lot of clapping after it. Miss Baxter rose to hand over the tea set. Miss Carson rose, too, a smiling pink-cheeked Miss Carson in a bright swirl of pink skirt. Her hands reached out to touch the tea set lying on the table between her and Miss Baxter; and after that, everything happened very fast.

Mr. Hargreave whipped a tuner from his pocket. As he blew it to get the note for their song the Earl strode to the window beside the platform, and all of Miss Carson's pupils rose in a body. They opened their mouths to sing at the same moment as the Earl threw up the bottom window sash and leaned out with a large white handkerchief waving from his hand.

"That's Tom that I hear . . ."

The first line of the song rang out. Miss Carson shook her head, smiling at the music, puzzled by the Earl's actions and by what she thought was a mistake in the words.

"He swings the big hammer . . ." Right on cue came the noise from the smithy, iron against iron, rattling, clanging, banging; a maelstrom of sound with men's voices mixed in it, cheering, shouting, laughing voices. They went on singing throughout the din, while the tempo of it became wilder and ever wilder; and inside the hall, the laughter that had started as a murmur grew into a great wave of sound. As their voices soared in the final glissando of the verse, Miss Carson put her hands over her ears. She was laughing, too, in a bewildered sort of way; and when they had finished, all she could do was to smile again and to shrug as she glanced from them to the noise still going on outside. That was when the Earl stepped forward, offering his arm to her as formally as if at some great ceremony.

"Miss Carson," he asked, "will you do me the honor?"

Miss Carson laid a hand on his arm, her look plainly asking what was to happen next. Mr. Hargreave shouted,

"All of Miss Carson's pupils fall in line directly behind her and the Earl. Anyone else who wants to, fall in behind them."

Nimbly, then, he leapt down from the platform. The Earl led Miss Carson to the floor of the hall and down the central aisle between the benches. Everyone followed behind these two, Miss Carson's pupils first, then the rest of the school, then the parents. And, led by Mr. Hargreave, they went in procession like this, down the lane to the smithy. The nearer they drew to it, too, the less became the noise from it. Some of the men standing around in the yard, laughing, and beating iron on iron, had seen them coming and had passed word along to the rest.

Archie Meikle was standing at the smithy door, leaning on his fourteen-pound hammer, dressed as usual in working clothes covered by his blacksmith's leather apron. As usual, too, his face was streaked with the dirt and sweat of a day in the smithy; but the expression beneath the dirt was a serious one, and when the Earl and Miss Carson stopped in front of him he stayed where he was, standing quite still in the doorway of his smithy.

It wasn't possible to see Miss Carson's face at that moment—not pent-up behind her and the Earl in that procession; but she was near enough to see Archie's face, and to hear him tell Miss Carson,

"Now don't you be feared, lassie, even although you've been taken by surprise like this. Your Tom's here, too, and we mean no harm."

Mr. Hargreave held up his hands for silence, and Archie cried out,

"Now all of you folks here that belong in Ballinford are acquainted with the law of this country. You know that a man and woman are truly married if, before two witnesses, they say that they do take one another in marriage. That's what we call 'a marriage by declaration.' And just because you are country folks, too, you know there's a certain tradition that has to do with such a marriage. But the young ones here don't know that tradition, and that's why I'm here now to explain it to them."

The smithy yard had gone very quiet. In the silence, Archie stood aside to let the Earl lead Miss Carson into the smithy. Then he took up his place in the doorway again, and with a sweep of his arm that brought them all closing in on him, he shouted,

"Now you young ones, see me here—Archie Meikle, master blacksmith. That's an important craft, the working of iron; the most important of all country crafts. And it always has been so. But marriage is important, too; and to last for a lifetime, a marriage must be made as strong as iron. That's the reason why, in long-ago days when there was no priest or minister handy, it was the custom for the village blacksmith to perform a marriage. And it's that old, old custom we're going to follow now, for the benefit of my son Tom, and his bride."

That was the strangest yet of all the moments in that strange day—listening to Archie Meikle, watching him as he spoke. A dignity had come over Archie as he stood there, over the squat powerfulness of his form, the lines of his swarthy face; and in the words he used, there was a sense of ancient things that sent a shiver up her spine. As he turned to enter the smithy she pressed eagerly forward to follow him, and the shiver became a feeling of tingling expectation.

Ahead of her, with the light from the doorway blocked by all those pushing from behind, she saw the interior of the smithy as a cave of shadow shot glowingly through by the red and gold of flames leaping in the forge fire. At the center of this flame-pierced dimness there was a figure in pink—Miss Carson, standing at one side of the big anvil. Facing Miss Carson from the opposite side of the anvil, stood Tom Meikle. Like Archie, Tom was in his working clothes, shirt sleeves rolled up, leather apron on, his face grimy. This part of it all was a complete surprise to him, too, she realized. Tom was a formal man, who liked things to be neat and orderly, and so he would be the very last to have a dirty face at his own wedding.

More and more people pressed in behind her. The smithy was becoming uncomfortably crowded, but all those nearest the anvil were still Miss Carson's pupils. The Earl and Mr. Hargreave saw to that, forming them into a ring, three deep, around her and Tom. Then Mr. Hargreave and the Earl themselves took up position, standing shoulder to shoulder and facing Archie across the length of the anvil, as Tom and Miss Carson were facing one another across the breadth of it. Archie lifted his fourteen-pound hammer and held it in a firm, two-handed grip. He looked from Tom to Miss Carson, and told them,

"Join hands across the anvil."

Miss Carson was pale now. Her lipstick was very bright against the paleness of her face. Slowly, looking at Tom all the time, she began raising her right hand. She was so much the smaller of the two that she had to keep looking upwards. Tom raised his hand to meet hers. Standing close to such a small woman, he seemed even taller than ever—and even more handsome, with the firelight gilding the strong lines of his face and shining ruddily on his fair head. Yet still, in spite of all that, there was a tremble in the big, work-darkened fingers of the hand that touched Miss Carson's.

Archie shot a quick glance at the Earl. Their eyes met. And the Earl was very serious now. The Earl also had a strong feeling for the old customs. The dark, lively glance and the pale, keen one signalled understanding to one another—or was it complicity? Had they planned together for it to be like this?

"Do you, Thomas Meikle, take this woman for your wedded wife?"

Archie's voice rang out firmly, stilling the little murmur that had followed the joining of hands. And just as firmly, Tom answered,

"I do."

"Do you, Marjorie Carson, take this man for your wedded husband?"

Miss Carson's reply came quietly, but clearly. "I do."

Archie raised his hammer high. "Then I, Archibald Meikle, blacksmith, declare you well and truly married."

On the word "married," the hammer came flashing downwards. It struck the anvil, just a hairsbreadth away from the clasped hands, and the sound of it was like a bell ringing release for all the pent-up feelings in the smithy. They burst out in a sigh, and a shout of congratulation. Tom leaned across the anvil to kiss the bride. Archie seized her, and kissed her also. Then it was the turn of the Earl and Mr. Hargreave; and when the laughter from all that died down, there was Archie grinning from ear to ear and triumphantly telling everyone,

"Well, that's it now. *And* they can still have their church wedding—ten church weddings, if they like. It won't make them any more man and wife than *I've* made them!"

9

Archie's voice was loud; as loud, Jinty
thought, as if she had heard him speaking right there
beside her in the Fiscal's waiting room instead of just in
her own memory of that day of the anvil-marriage.
With her wandering mind thus abruptly brought back
to present reality, she stopped staring into space to look
directly at him instead; and as soon as she did so, she
realized he had indeed just finished speaking. His
hunched position was straightened. In one hand he
held the heavy gold watch that usually lay in a pocket
of his waistcoat, with its chain festooned across the
waistcoat front. He was frowning down towards the
face of the watch; and, as if confirming the remark he
had made the moment before her eyes lit on him, he
slid the watch back into its pocket and announced,

"Aye. By my reckoning he's had Garvald in there
with him a good half hour now."

The sound of Archie's words vanished into the studied

silence her mother had imposed on the room, and once again Jinty felt the embarrassment that had gripped her when his greeting to them had been ignored. There was a clock high on the wall opposite her chair. With the vague notion of showing Archie that she, at least, had paid attention to him, she glanced at the clock as if checking his watch with the time it gave. The clock had stopped. Its hands stood at half past eight. *Half past eight—the time the school bus left the village for Haimston and the Academy* . . . She stared at the clock, unseeingly, her mind's eye providing instead a picture of herself travelling for the first time on that bus.

The change that her first year at the Academy had meant for her, she realized then, had been the biggest one in her life so far. And it hadn't just been due, either, to the Academy being so big and strange after the familiar atmosphere of the small village school. Nor had it been only a matter of mastering the timetabled routine for the many new subjects in senior school, or the sprawling geography of its various classrooms. There had been so much of other and different sorts of things she'd had to learn, apart from all that.

The fact that she'd done nothing brilliant, after all, in passing the Quali—that, once she'd discovered herself to be just a mote in a crowd of new pupils from other village schools, had been the first of them. Then had come the business of trying to accustom herself to seeing Linda and Meg as the rest of the school saw them—Linda, the clever one, so good at maths that she could argue with the Head Maths Master himself; Meg, the popular all-rounder, with as good a record on the sports field as in the classroom. That had been one side of seeing her sisters in their familiar world that was so strange to her; the side she had expected to see. But the other side—the one that was only possible because the Academy was not in the village and under their mother's eye—that was the one that had taken her by surprise and really changed things for her.

There were fashions at the Academy. That had been the beginning of her insight into the other side of Linda's life there; and it was Linda herself who set these fashions. The new ways she found to wear her school hat and school scarf, her walk, her gestures, the poses she struck—all the junior girls and most of the senior ones, too, were envious of the sophisticated air these things gave to Linda; and so they copied her, trying themselves to be as cool and worldly-wise as she seemed to be. But with Meg it was different, because Meg didn't care whether she was fashionable or not; and the other side to Meg's life at the Academy was Dave Ferguson. Meg and Dave were courting. Dave worked in a garage at Haimston, and being at the Academy gave Meg the chance to meet him without their mother knowing about it.

Jinty stole a glance at the face beside her; the quiet, self-contained face her mother always showed to the outside world. For a moment or two then, she wondered at the courage of endurance that lay hidden under the mask of its thin features; but coming hard on this, another and older form of wondering asserted itself.

How was it that her mother, who took such an interest in all their days at school, had never noticed the effect these meetings had had on Meg? How had she failed to see the radiance each one of them left on Meg's face, or to guess from that about the inner glow they had lit? And as for herself, how on earth had she ever managed to keep the secret of them from her mother? Especially so in that first year at the Academy when the knowledge that she was now part of a conspiracy of silence had been so fresh in her mind?

Archie Meikle stirred restlessly. He looked at his watch again, gave an impatient click of his tongue, and muttered something about "all this damned waiting." He looked across the room, a glint of calculation in his eye; then, unexpectedly, he asked,

"How d'you feel about it, Jinty? Waiting around like this to answer a lot of questions?"

Jinty looked at her mother, more than half expecting she would forbid an answer to Archie's question; but there was no change in her mother's look of quiet reserve, no words from her.

"Come on, Jinty," Archie encouraged. "We've sat like dummies long enough, haven't we? How *do* you feel?"

"A bit nervous," Jinty told him; and added cautiously, "because I've never been a witness before, I suppose."

"You're no different from myself, then," Archie remarked. "And Mr. Talbot—the Fiscal—he's not a bad chap, you know; but they say he's shrewd, for all that.

And the way he's arranged things today, I can believe it."

With a meaning little nod that seemed to confirm the vague threat in his words, Archie sat back, waiting for her to answer. She looked at him, not knowing how to give shape to the questions it had roused in her mind, and then was startled to hear her mother abruptly demanding,

"What are you hinting at, Archie Meikle?"

"Well, since you ask," Archie began, and from his air of elaborate politeness then, Jinty began to think that talking to her had been no more than a device to draw her mother into conversation. "Since you ask, Mrs. Morrison, I'll remind you that all three of us—Lord Garvald, myself, and Jinty—have already been interviewed by the police. Isn't that so?"

"We all know that's so. I asked what you were hinting at."

"Quite, quite," Archie agreed. "And I was just going to remind you that, on the night the Earl died, the police interviewed scores of people. They had to, you'll remember, considering how the public nature of the occasion then meant that any one of them might have noticed something of importance. And so why d'you think the Procurator has chosen to give his personal attention to only three now, out of all that lot?"

"I know why he wants to see me!" Jinty blurted the words out in a voice that she realized had become strangely thick and breathless; and once again, her mother intervened for her.

"Jinty," she said sharply, "was the last person to speak to the Earl before he died. You know that even better than I do. And so you know perfectly well, too, what makes her evidence important enough for the Fiscal's personal attention."

"Of course," Archie agreed. "We all realize that. But why me, as well? And why Lord Garvald? Why all three of us, *one right after the other*?"

Neither Jinty nor her mother answered, although he gave them time to do so; and eventually he went on.

"The Fiscal has wide powers, you know, and he doesn't have to hold himself to the kind of questions a policeman might ask. If he thinks it could have a bearing on the case, he can probe into any part of a person's life. And if you ask me, that's what he's doing now with Lord Garvald. He's getting out of that young man a picture of the way *he* saw the Earl—the son's picture. And when it comes to my turn, he'll not only question me about all the long conversation I had with the Earl that night. He'll also try to get from me a picture of how I—his friend—saw him."

Archie paused for a moment; and then, with a look that defied them to challenge the words, he added, "His best friend, don't forget. And once the Fiscal's done that, he'll put it together with what Jinty has to say, to make one complete picture. You mark my words. That'll be both the order and the style of these interviews. And that's how the Fiscal will finally arrive at his decision."

"His decision on what?" Jinty asked, and thought as

she spoke how ignorant she must sound. But she still had to know, because how otherwise could she make her own final decision—the one that would dictate how much she could afford to tell the Fiscal, or how much she would have to conceal from him?

"On whether the inquiry will stop here, of course," Archie said, "or whether it will have to go on to being a public affair."

"A *public affair*"—with that fearsome oath to be taken! Through dry lips, Jinty asked the question that was at the root of all her anxiety over the interview ahead of her.

"Mr. Meikle, supposing the Fiscal asks me if the Earl said anything to me about the Ballinford doom. What'll I tell him?"

Archie's lips shaped themselves for an answer, but before he could utter a sound, her mother cut in,

"That'll do, Archie Meikle. I've sat here long enough hearing you go roundabout to try putting words into Jinty's mouth."

Archie clamped his lips firmly shut again. Then, with a sigh and a shrug of exasperation, he said, "Have it your own way, Mistress Morrison—as you have had from the beginning of this business, of course. She's your daughter, after all."

"And the Earl was my friend as well as yours," her mother retorted.

There was a moment of hostile silence while her mother and Archie sat glaring at one another; then Archie's eyes broke away as the woman clerk who had shown them into the waiting room passed by the open door and he became aware of her moving presence. Head swiftly turning, he called after her,

"Hey, missis!"

"Yes?" The clerk stopped, glancing back towards him with a look that showed she was not too well pleased by the countrified title he had given her.

"How much longer?" Archie demanded. "I've got a smithy that needs tending, I'd have you know—Fiscal or no Fiscal!"

"I'll—I'll inquire." The clerk's uncertain tones showed how flustered she had become in the face of Archie's peremptory manner. But she did her best, all the same, going straightaway to knock on the Fiscal's door, sticking her head around it to say something in a low voice, and then coming back to report,

"A few minutes more, Mr. Meikle, and Mr. Talbot will be ready for you."

"Aye. It's not before time," Archie told her, seemingly only a little mollified; but when she had hurried off again, he grinned and said to the room at large, "That put life into the silly besom!"

Something of the tension in Jinty exploded with the remark. She laughed out loud at it, and Archie told her,

"That's better. I thought for a while there that you'd suddenly been struck dumb by all this business."

"I was thinking," she said. "I've got a lot to think about, Mr. Meikle."

"So have we all," Archie told her soberly. "So have we all."

They sat in silence again after that until Archie asked her—absently, as if searching around for something to keep the conversation going,

"And how's life treating you apart from all this, Jinty? Still doing well at the Academy, are you?"

"Not all that well," she told him, and hoped her mother would still be so intent on not speaking to Archie that no contradiction would be forthcoming. "Some of the subjects—like maths and physics, you know—are hard to do. And I was never one of the brainy ones."

"Jinty!" The sudden reproach in her mother's voice warned her that the hope had been in vain. And then it came, the boast that always had to be made to prove it wasn't possible for one of the Morrison girls *not* to be doing well at the Academy. "Art is Jinty's best subject. She's *very* good at art."

"Well, well!" Archie tried to sound impressed. "So you'll be a famous artist someday, will you?"

That was the kind of thing her mother liked people to say. And a quick shake of the head to deny it—that was the only kind of answer she could possibly give, because it wasn't like that for her in the art class; nothing like that at all, in spite of the high marks she got there. Everything she did in art class, in fact, was odd, wrong, different somehow, from the way it was supposed to be.

"Jinty, cabbages are green. Why have you painted them this peculiar color?"

"Because that's the way they are, Mr. Verity, sir."

Livid, bluish-green, with veins that seemed swollen to bursting-point, crawling all over the leaves.

"*And the line, Jinty, the line! A cabbage grows straight up from its stem, doesn't it?*"

"*No, sir. It bends a little.*" Like a big, unwieldy head. A whole field of blue-green heads sadly drooping.

"*Well, I'm only an art teacher, not an agricultural expert, and so I'll grant you that landscape. But what about this painting; the one that was supposed to be called 'A Summer's Day'? You've got nothing here except a great swirl of gold, like the track of a wind blowing all around this small figure with the blind eyes— this here; the dancing figure dressed like a clown. No trees, no grass, no flowers, no clouds; nothing at all except that.*"

"*Yes, sir. But, sir, if the clown can't see the day, that's how it is for him—just the wind, the warm gold wind. And dancing about in it; enjoying it the only way he knows.*"

"*Ah, yes. Um—tell me something, Jinty. Do you know that all human beings are supposed to have the vestiges of a third eye; an eye which senses, rather than sees?*"

"*I've never heard of it, sir.*"

"*I'm not surprised. One encounters the representation of it mostly in Eastern art. But it is still this third eye perception which lies behind any effort at giving physical form to some inner experience; as, for instance, may have been the case here with you, in what could be an attempt to portray the connection between the isolation of the blind and the loneliness of the clown. That's why I'm not only going to allow these paintings to pass. I'm also going to give them a good mark; a really high mark."*

"But, sir, I can't draw."

"How right you are, Jinty. You do have a strong sense of color, I admit, but your draftsmanship is poor. You'll never be an artist, my girl. Nevertheless, it seems to me that your third eye perception is keener than normal, and that I should therefore allow my marking system to encourage it. Furthermore, I advise you to cultivate it in your own way. And if—as seems to be the case—it relates particularly to people, you will eventually find your true bent."

Mr. Verity said some peculiar things. Mr. Verity needed his head examined, they said. But although she had her own thoughts on that score, she still knew that the kind of marks he gave her would never be of any practical use. Everybody knew that, in fact; everybody except her mother, building a career for her out of one classmark on her report card, taking the end result of it for granted, trying to shape her whole life around it—just as she had done with Linda's report card, and with Meg's!

The door of the Fiscal's office began to open. Jinty looked up, at the squeaking sound it made, and realized that a conversation between her mother and Archie Meikle had been flowing around her—to judge by their faces, a conversation that had angered both of them. The opening door drew their glances away from one another. Then, as the figure of Lord Garvald became visible within the narrow view they now had of the office beyond the door, Archie said urgently,

"Look, we've only seconds left before the next interview, and I've got to make you understand. It's only your pride that's keeping you and Meg apart now. And that's stupid, when your heart is breaking for her as much as hers is breaking for you."

Jinty began her familiar silent prayer. *"Please, Mam, forgive Meg. Please forgive her. Please!"*

The silent urging had no more effect than Archie's spoken plea, and her mother's voice was bitter as she said,

"You've got a right to talk, I suppose—you that encouraged Dave Ferguson around the smithy in the first place, and loaned him money, and—"

"Now here!" Archie interrupted. "That's not true! It was always Tom he came to see—never me. And the money wasn't for Dave's benefit. I loaned it to safeguard Tom's future."

"And what about Meg's future?" This was the real nub of the argument, and the bitterness had an even sharper edge. "It wasn't just cash you gave the Ferguson fellow. It was ideas too; the ideas he put into my girl's head."

"You're havering, woman," Archie protested. "Your Meg didn't need to be told something that was common knowledge in the village. *And* she didn't need anyone to make up her mind, either, when she decided to act on it."

"She was too young to know what she was doing."

"She was seventeen."

"Aye, seventeen. A mere girl! And you were the one that made it possible, instead of trying to stop her as you should have done."

"Meg was of age—a year over the legal age. And damned well you know I could no more have stopped her than I could have stopped the sun rising!"

The office door swung wide open, with a rush of voices from it sounding over Archie's final words. Mr. Talbot, the Fiscal, came out into the corridor with Lord Garvald following him. As they emerged, both Jinty and her mother looked away from Archie, and towards them. Archie swung around, to follow the direction of their look. The Fiscal caught his eye, and said,

"Oh yes, Mr. Meikle. Just go right into my office, will you, please? I'll be with you in a moment."

Side by side with Lord Garvald, then, the Fiscal moved slowly off down the corridor. Archie took a couple of steps towards the waiting room door, hesitated, then looked back as if about to say some parting word; and on an impulse stronger than any apprehension of her mother's disapproval, Jinty said rapidly,

"Mr. Meikle, I don't blame you about Meg. And I don't blame Tom, either, or Miss Car—young Mrs. Tom."

"I know that, Jinty." All the anger had gone out of Archie's face. His voice was quiet now. His gaze travelled beyond her, and reached her mother. "And Mrs.

Morrison, I'm sorry I lost my temper with you, but—"

"It'll be Jinty's turn in there next," her mother interrupted the apology, "and so there's just one more thing I have to say. You spoke yourself about the way the Fiscal will probe around until he can build up his own picture of the Earl. And so I'm warning you now. Don't you shame me by repeating anything you've learned about me and my family. You've done enough harm as it is, without adding that to it."

Archie shook his head. "I wish you could see it," he said. "You've harmed yourself already, more than I could ever do."

They watched him disappearing into the Fiscal's office before they settled down again, with her mother saying,

"He doesn't know what he's talking about, blaming me. Was it my fault that Meg took the law into her own hands?"

She sounded like someone fighting a losing battle with herself, Jinty thought, but closed her mouth on the temptation to say so; and after a moment, her mother said,

"All right, don't bother to tell me. I know how you feel about Meg."

The sound of footsteps outside the waiting room door and then the sight of Mr. Talbot hurrying back into his office, held them both momentarily silent. Jinty wandered over to one of the tall windows overlooking the open space of Market Square. The Rolls was still in its parking place outside the Sheriff Court, but now there was a figure in the driver's seat. John Ferguson, the chauffeur, had returned from wherever he had spent the time of Lord Garvald's interview. With her gaze coming to rest on Ferguson's squarely-set back, Jinty heard her mother continuing,

"And Linda? What about her? I suppose Archie Meikle could twist what she did, so that I was to blame for her as well. And you that's so friendly with him—you'd agree with that too, wouldn't you?"

"No!" Jinty spoke to the space outside the window, surprising even herself with the vehemence of her tone. "Linda was different. It hurt Meg when she had to hurt you. But Linda was cruel. Linda *used* you to get what she wanted. And me, too. *And* the Earl."

Lord Garvald came out of the Sheriff Court Building. He ran down the steps towards the Rolls, slid into the front passenger seat, and the chauffeur began easing the car away from the steps. Head bent to watch its progress, and only half aware of movement behind her, Jinty heard her mother's voice sounding hesitantly at her shoulder.

"Jinty—the um, the Ballinford doom? What made you speak to Archie Meikle about it the way you did?"

"Because—" She checked the answer that had been on the tip of her tongue and changed it to "I can't tell you."

"Why not? I'm your mother. I *should* know."

"Oh, please!" Turning so quickly on the words that the two of them collided, shoulder to shoulder, she burst out, "Archie couldn't have told me what to say, anyway. And you can't either. Nobody could, except the Earl, and he's dead. So leave me alone, will you, Mam? Please!"

"I was only trying to help you. You're too young to realize—"

"No, Mam, I'm not too young. That's the whole trouble. That's why you've got to let me do this thing my own way." Facing windowwards again and edging away from the too-close contact with her mother, Jinty added silently, *"Like you should have done with Meg and Linda."*

"You're thrawn. I've always said that. You've got a contrary streak in you. And God help me, you're every bit as stubborn as your sisters."

Her mother had gone back to her seat with the words. Jinty spared a glance for her, and had to steel herself to turn away again. Her mother looked old, defeated, like she had on the night of the great burst-up with Meg and Linda. But that also was part of the pattern, wasn't it? And she *had* to get the whole of it straight in her mind before she was questioned by the Fiscal.

The Rolls was out in the stream of traffic now. If she could follow it with her mind, as she was following it with her eyes . . . ! Where would that take her?

10

She was back again at harvest time. But she was older now—two years older than she had been when Meg sneaked out to the kirn. The Rolls was parked at the gate into the churchyard. There was dust on the gleam of its coachwork, because it was the Earl who sat behind the wheel and he always drove fast.

It was Sunday, the day of Mr. Elphinston's harvest-home service, and the two figures ahead of her on the path into church were Lord Garvald and Lady Stane-ford, his aunt. Nobody else from Ballinford Hall ever came to Mr. Elphinston's church. They went to big, fancy churches in Edinburgh, instead. But these two always came; and it was always the Earl who drove them, because Sunday was John Ferguson's day off from chauffeuring.

Trailing into church behind her mother and Meg and Linda she turned for a last glance at the car. Its folding canvas top was rolled back. The Earl was sprawling with his arm across the back of the driver's seat, one leg cocked over the low door on that side, eyes closed, face upturned to the morning sun. He looked half asleep, but the careless pose was only a mask for impatience at having to sit there. That was something she knew from experience, and she went into church wondering if this was to be one of the occasions when his impatience would get the better of him.

Inside the church, color blazed out at her from the harvest decorations, and the air compounded from their scents seemed rich enough to eat. There were no flowers, of course, because—Mr. Elphinston said—flowers were frivolous things to bring into God's house. But there were sheaves of barley glowing gold against the altar. Marrows as fat as pigs, and big crinkle-leaved cabbages, made heaps of greeny-yellow and bluish-green in front of the gold. The smaller heaps of pinkish-gold and shining scarlet were peaches from the Earl's greenhouses and apples from his orchard; and the huge mound that almost hid little Miss Fairlie the organist from view, was made of turnips piled up in a mass of smooth and solid purple.

"We plow the fields and scatter/The good seed on the land—"

The church was full. Everybody seemed to have recovered from the sore heads that had followed from the kirn on Friday night, and everybody sang, but mostly it was the wobbly sweetness of the women's voices that came through.

"But it is fed and watered/By God's almighty hand—"

She forced volume from her own voice, enjoying the power of the alto notes that had come into it ever since the flowers had finally visited her.

"He sends the snow in winter/The warmth to swell the grain—"

There was Mrs. Tom Meikle looking as if she would have her baby any day now. And if Dave Ferguson wasn't a lot more careful, her mother would be sure to notice the way he kept glancing at Meg, instead of at his hymnbook.

"The breezes and the sunshine/And soft, refreshing rain—"

That barley against the altar had been the very last of harvest at the Mains; the part that was always cut by hand because of all the hares the reaper had driven inwards to take refuge in it. But there was one sheaf missing from it now—the corn dolly sheaf.

"All good gifts around us/Are sent from Heav'n above/Then thank the Lord, O thank the Lord/For a-a-all His love."

A chorus. She liked a hymn with a chorus. She sang the final repeat of it in her loudest voice; but it was still the barley sheaves that had first place in her mind, and as the hymn finished with Mr. Elphinston preparing to read the first lesson, she let her thoughts escape entirely to them.

It had been early evening when they cut those last sheaves of harvest. They always did leave that job till the evening, so that as many folk as possible could be there; but the sun was still high, and striking brightly off the single patch of barley left standing at the center of the field. The reaper that had cut the rest of the field lay idle, with Dave Ferguson tinkering away at something in its engine. It was Dave who serviced all the farm machinery, now that he had finished his apprenticeship at the garage in Haimston. Meg was leaning on the reaper, talking to him, smiling often at the things he said in answer. But Linda hadn't come to the field. Linda looked down her nose, nowadays, at everything to do with the village.

The field itself had a great air of expectancy about it. Even the kids there had stopped their chasing and running. The people laughing and talking to one another had a waiting look. The corn dolly would be made from the very last of all the sheaves to be cut from that standing barley, and then it would be hung inside the barn at the Mains—for a charm, they said, to protect the crops there all through the coming winter. And that was important. The hares that would run out of the barley were important too. Hares were food, of course, but there was also something about the excitement of killing the last hares of harvest that seemed to make them special in the same way as the last of harvest itself was special.

Mrs. Torrie went past her to join the women reapers standing ready with their sickles. It was Mrs. Torrie who would get the job of making the corn dolly. She was good at that. Then, when Alec took the first horse out for the first plowing of another year, Mrs. Torrie would bring the dolly from the barn to give to the horse for a sweet bite. The dung from the sweet bite would drop onto the field, and when that dung had been plowed into the ground, they could be sure of another harvest.

That was something else people said. That was how it had always gone at the Mains; and even although she was seeing it all now through the eyes of a whole year's experience at the Academy, the ritual feeling in it was still sending prickles of excitement over her skin.

Dave Ferguson and Meg came to stand beside her. They walked hand in hand. Meg had a glow on her, like a flower in bloom, and Dave was more than ever like her own private idea of the Dashing White Sergeant, but she still had no more than a glance for them. They spoke to her, but she didn't answer. She was too intent on watching the Earl, waiting for him to give the signal for the start of the reaping.

He was away to her right, among the men who would kill the hares, laughing and joking with them about the fine time everyone would have at the kirn that night. The kirn . . . It was something they weren't even allowed to mention at home now, never mind being banned from taking part in it! The men were all armed with heavy sticks; and gradually, as she watched, they began to fan out into a wide circle around the patch of standing barley. The boys in the field rushed to join them. Boys always seemed to be keen to join in the slaughter of the hares.

The women reapers also had their eyes fixed on the

Earl. He raised one hand, brought it down again sharply; and they bent to the barley, their sickles rising and falling against it. Swift—their cutting motions were swift, with random flashes of sun striking off the curved sickle blades. The hares began darting out from their dwindling patch of cover, eyes bulging with panic, brown-gray bodies at full stretch.

The sticks flailed out at them. The field became a bedlam of shouts, yells, curses, shot through with the screams of hares that had been wounded by a first blow and needed a second one to dispatch them. Blood spurted—hares always seemed to bleed freely. There was her own father, with a great smear of it on his shirt.

She shrank from it all, repelled by the blood and the dying screams. And yet it didn't last. Just one great explosion of violence, and it was all over. The hares were dead, the women were standing with their arms full of harvest sheaves. And there was a sense of rightness in the air—a satisfying sort of feeling, as if something that was proper and necessary had been accomplished.

The Earl had moved to stand among the women reapers. He seemed even more massive with his size contrasted against theirs. Mrs. Torrie was close beside him, her pudgy face scarlet with effort, but still beaming pleasure up at him. One of the women handed him a sheaf of barley, the very last one to be cut; the corn dolly sheaf. He shouted to the men. They paused in their work of gathering up the limp bodies of the hares, and straightened up to look towards him. He held the sheaf high for them to see, triumphantly poising it at the stretch of one long arm; and for the moment the gesture lasted, something deep in her responded to it with the same sense of elemental triumph. Corn dolly was safe! There would be another harvest.

The moment broke with his dropping the sheaf down towards the eager grasp of Mrs. Torrie's hands. Yet still that view of the Earl holding it was there in her mind like a picture, with the field's golden stubble for its frame; and still it was that picture she could see now imposed on the one made by Mr. Elphinston standing in front of the barley in church, to announce the next hymn.

Rustle, rustle, rustle, as they all rose to sing. People coughing and clearing their throats, and the same again when it was all over. Mr. Elphinston began to pray. Mr. Elphinston believed in extemporary prayer, and he loved the sound of his own voice. How awful to be God and to *have* to listen to him. More reading, more singing, more prayer. Peering through her fingers at the heaped-up red of the apples, she felt her sweet tooth aching to bite into one of them. *"Gentle Jesus, let me have an apple—"* but gentle Jesus didn't stand a chance against the bloody-eyed and vengeful God that Mr. Elphinston prayed to; which was a pity, because fruit was so expensive that they hardly ever had it at home.

"All things living He doth feed/His full hand supplies their need—"

Mr. Elphinston was in the pulpit now, and he had taken lines from the second hymn for the text of his

135

sermon. He said them quietly, paused, and frowned. The pause stretched out until suddenly, in a great roar of sound, he gave out the lines again; and immediately then she knew what the theme of his sermon would be. Hell. Mr. Elphinston was getting ready for another of his warnings that they would all land up in hell if they didn't do as *he* said.

"As if he had a private key to the place," she thought resentfully.

"*His* full hand," Mr. Elphinston insisted. "The fount, the source of these, our harvest blessings, is the hand of Almighty God. It is *not* the pagan fertility symbol called the corn dolly. Neither is it the dung that Alec Torrie's Clydesdales drop, after they have chewed their way through that heathen abomination. That, my friends is a belief to be stamped on in this parish, as it should be throughout the whole country. To God the glory, I say. And for any of you to say otherwise would be blasphemy—the sheerest blasphemy."

Mr. Elphinston was always going on about blasphemy. And why did he say "my friends" when he was glaring so angrily at everybody? It wasn't as if there was any harm, after all, in the little corn dolly— "*corn dolly, corn dolly . . .*" In an effort to shut out the sound of Mr. Elphinston's voice booming away at the words, she fixed her eyes again on the shining red of the apples, and deliberately began thinking of the last time she had been one of a village gang raiding the Earl's orchard.

. . . the fence, the high spiked fence! Balancing on top of it, and the heart-stopping moment of the leap that took her clear of the spikes to land in the orchard on the other side. Running through the trees, and as she ran, growing dizzy from looking up to their canopy of silvery-green leaves studded with the red blobs of apples. The noise of other running feet on every side of her. The silver-green canopy bending and shaking, the red apples raining down—sweet, honey-sweet apples! And afterwards, in the grassy place where they hid the spoils, laughing with the others over the raid, rolling about and wrestling with them like a litter of puppies playing, her mouth spluttering-full of the honey-sweet pith, in her nostrils the heady smell of crushed grass and apples and the warm bodies tussling with her own.

Harvest home, harvest home . . . All the time she was part of that warm, laughing struggle, she could hear the words beating in her mind with the compulsive liveliness of a kirn tune. And she could see them, as well as hear them; huge words written right across her inward vision in Gothic letters like those at the beginning of each paragraph in the big Bible on the church lectern, and every letter blazing brilliant with color. Blue and red and gold and green and silver—the colors were those of sky and apples and sun and grass and leafy canopies, all interlaced and sweeping across her mind in a great shining shout of harvest praise. And although she had no idea whether she was praising Mr. Elphinston's hell-fire God or the pagan

137

something in the corn dolly, the glory of the shout filled her mind so completely that she did not care either. . . .

"Dr-r-r-ink!" Mr. Elphinston's voice crashed into her mind again with a single word stretched out over a long, rolling "r" sound. She tried to resist it, yet still found the boom of it reverberating in every corner of her mind. He was preaching now, about the kirn; swaying back and forward in the pulpit, thumbs hooked into the armholes of his robe, eyebrows furiously twitching up and down his forehead, and gradually she became fascinated by the way those eyebrows moved in time to individual words

"Yes, dr-r-r-ink, my friends," Mr. Elphinston roared. "There is dr-r-ink taken at the kir-r-n. And what is the twin evil of that? Aye, well do I ask!"

Mr. Elphinston paused as if gathering the combined forces of voice, glaring eyes, and twitching eyebrows for one final assault on their attention; and then, leaning right forward over the front of the pulpit, he delivered the full blast of it at them.

"For-r-r-nication!"

That did it! Laughter, the awful irrepressible tide of laughter that had been building up inside her, began leaking out in a series of choking sounds. She groped for a handkerchief to stifle them, heard other sounds beside her, and became aware of Meg and Linda sitting crimson-faced in the attempt to suppress their own laughter. Immediately the awful force inside herself grew stronger; and she bowed her head, too occupied with fighting it now to hear another word of the sermon.

"In the Name of the Father, the Son, and the Holy Ghost," Mr. Elphinston finished sternly at last. Two sidesmen arose, holding plates for the offering; and with relief, as she reached for her Sunday penny to add to the collection, she was finally able to regain control of herself.

Lord Garvald was one of the sidesmen. He smiled at people as he passed the plate along the pews, a shy sort of smile that seemed to show he wanted people to like him. She watched him going back down the aisle, tall like his father, but still lacking his father's breadth, and wondered what it was like to be Lord Garvald who could pick a peach or an apple whenever he fancied one. For a moment, she envied him with a fierce, overwhelming envy. Then she remembered the Ballinford doom, and was glad to be a village brat who could not get apples except by stealing them.

"*Come ye thankful people come/Raise the song of harvest home. . . .*" They had reached the closing hymn, everybody singing away at it as serious and long-faced as Mr. Elphinston himself—not the same folk at all, to look at them now, as the ones that had danced their feet off at the kirn on Friday night. "*All is safely gathered in/Ere the winter storms begin. . . .*" Flowery hats on the women, men's necks bulging from stiff, high collars. "*God our Maker will provide . . .*" Not the corn dolly. Not the dung from Alec Torrie's horses. Heathen, that was heathen. "*For our wants to be supplied . . .*" Could people wear flowery hats and stiff collars to sing in church and still be heathen? *"Come to God's own temple, come . . ."* Women with paper streamers entangled in their hair. Men dancing in tackety boots, collars gaping open, mouths roaring out kirn tunes. *"Raise the song of—"* And there it went—the blast from the horn of the Rolls-Royce, breaking into the closing hymn as it always did when the Earl decided that the service had gone on for too long!

It wasn't as if he honked just the once, either. The noise persisted, as usual, right to the end of the hymn; and as usual, Miss Fairlie became so flustered by it that she struck one sour note after another on the organ. Mr. Elphinston flushed scarlet, huffing out his cheeks with rage until his face above his clerical collar was like a red balloon tied at one end with a piece of white tape. And of course, he couldn't say the blessing quietly, the way it was meant to be said.

"Lord, lettest now Thy servant depart in peace—" He had to bellow the whole thing out against the sound of the car horn—*roar, honk, roar, honk, roar, honk!* And this time, she realized, it just wasn't going to be possible to hold in her laughter.

Meg and Linda caught the infection from her. All three of them stood choking and spluttering, with hymnbooks raised to mask their faces. But Mr. Elphinston had seen them. Mr. Elphinston was leaning over the pulpit to denounce them, yelling at them for profaning God's house; and with fingers closing around her arm like a vise, her mother was preparing to hustle her out of church.

Miss Fairlie struck up a stumbled version of her usual organ voluntary, but instead of retiring to the vestry as was usual for him at that point, Mr. Elphinston went striding down the center aisle towards the front door of the church. There was a rush to follow him, with everyone immediately guessing at his intention of confronting the Earl; and all the bodies that blocked the aisle then, made a quick exit from church impossible after all.

II

"You needn't think this will let you get away with it, Jinty," her mother warned as they edged their way to the door. "Affronting me like that, before half the village!"

"I couldn't help it, Mam. Really, I couldn't."

It was the only excuse she had, of course, but it was still a feeble one; and even as she offered it, she was pinning her hope of reprieve on the thought that the coming battle might give her mother's annoyance time to cool. That interruption to the end of the service, after all, was a really sore point with Mr. Elphinston, and already it had caused plenty of trouble between him and the Earl. But this had always been the discreet kind of row that took place behind closed doors, whereas the open one that was threatened now looked like being the daddy of them all!

Her hopes rose as she realized that even her mother's

determination would not be enough to get them through the crowd gathered around Mr. Elphinston at the church gate. She edged her way to the churchyard railings, to a place that gave her a view of what was happening, and saw that Lord Garvald and Lady Staneford had got out ahead of the rest of the congregation. They were in the back seat of the Rolls, with the Earl closing the door on them while Mr. Elphinston yelled at him,

"You have profaned the Sabbath, my lord, raising a racket like that outside my church. You are in breach of God's law, I tell you, and a shame to this parish."

"Oh, come now, Elphinston!" The Earl was clearly not the least upset at Mr. Elphinston's ranting. He was grinning, in fact, seemingly quite delighted at the commotion he had caused. "You don't expect me to wait here forever, do you, with my lunch spoiling at home?"

"For goodness' sake, then," Mr. Elphinston roared, "if you haven't the patience to wait for Lord Garvald, why don't you let him drive himself to church?"

The grin on the Earl's face froze, on the instant, into something more like a snarl. "Or why don't you preach shorter sermons?" Harshly he flung the challenge out; and then, before Mr. Elphinston could even draw the breath to answer it, he was shouting, "You know why, Elphinston. You know bloody well that Garvald's not allowed to drive this car or any other."

"And whose fault is that? Have I not warned you that God's word says the sins of the fathers will be visited on the children? Here, in this very churchyard, have I not told you that the doom on your family is God's will, working through the centuries to punish sin?"

Mr. Elphinston had his breath now, and he was evidently launched on a tirade; but the Earl was the last person to stand and be lectured.

"And if *that's* your God," he roared, "can any decent man wonder if I want none of him? But you don't worship God, Elphinston. You worship religion! And that's something I'll toot my horn at any day of the week—Sunday included."

"Then may I live to see you damned as you deserve!" Mr. Elphinston shouted. "You, to stand there and talk to me about what is and what isn't decent. You, that has not only all your own sins to answer for, but other folks' sins as well, the way you encourage the people here to idolatrous practices like the corn dolly, and the wanton disgrace they call the kirn. They would all die a natural death, these things, if it weren't for that encouragement. And as minister of this parish, I tell you now that other souls will burn in hell yet, because of you!"

The Earl said nothing for a moment. Then he turned to get into the Rolls; and quietly now, speaking from the driver's seat there, he told the minister,

"Elphinston, you can hold a million harvest-home services, but you'd still be no different from the dry, narrow creature you are; still no nearer to understanding what custom and tradition can mean to folk of the land. You talk of the kirn, and throw out words like 'wanton.' But when was the last time you allowed yourself to think of the wonder in the sweet flowering of lovers' bodies? You put bread in your mouth every day, but what do you know of the pain and sweat needed to bring forth even the one sheaf that makes corn dolly? What do you know, either, of the feeling in the blood at such a triumph? But all of these are the very things plowed back into the earth with the plowing-back of corn dolly. And they're all sowing, Elphinston. They're all harvest. They're all God. And God help any man who has never felt it so!"

He was away, on the almost soundless purring of the car before anyone had recovered from the effect of his words. There was just one glimpse of his back-seat passengers—Lady Staneford's face hidden by her veil, Lord Garvald's face twisted by some torment private to himself; and then, as Mr. Elphinston brusquely thrust his way back to the church, they were all talking and exclaiming over the form the row had taken.

"Aye, he's a right clever old bugger, the Earl," Alec Torrie said admiringly. "Did you hear him there—the case he made out for corn dolly?"

There were nods and smiles at this; but it wasn't everyone in the village who went to the kirn or who thought the way Alec did, and Miss Armitage, the postmistress, was the one to speak up for these.

"For shame, you," she told Alec, "swearing like that on the Sabbath. Forbye, whatever *you* might think of the argument, it's my opinion that Mr. Elphinston had the right of it."

"He was certainly right about one thing," Tom Meikle

remarked, and everyone stared at this, wondering why a Meikle should suddenly agree with the minister, for a change. "I mean about old customs dying a natural death," Tom explained. "And I'm the one who knows *that*, considering there won't be much future for me as a village blacksmith once all the farms have given up horses for the plowing and changed over to tractors instead. As they must, you know. As they must soon."

Patie Anderson, the shepherd, winked and grinned in Alec's direction. "You hear that, Alec?" he asked. "And you can't feed corn dolly to a tractor—now, can you?"

There was laughter at Alec's expense, then. The crowd began to form into smaller groups, all breaking slowly away from the gate, and from the surge of movement this created, a voice called,

"Jinty, where *are* you?"

She looked around from her place at the fence. There were her mother and Linda, moving clear of the crowd, looking this way and that in search of her. And oh, the foolishness of it! There, too, were Meg and Dave Ferguson, stealing a meeting with one another under cover of all the turmoil that had been going on. They stood face to face, only half hidden by the angle of the church wall. Dave had his hands linked together behind Meg's back, so that his arms encircled her waist. They were talking, laughing, nuzzling one another's faces, quite unaware that the crowd was scattering and that there was nothing left now to disguise the fact of their meeting.

"*Meg—!*" Her mother had also spotted them, and the breathless outrage in the cry that announced this was enough to tell her what would happen next. There would be no room in her mother's mind now for anything so petty as laughter in church—not in the face of this kind of situation! With the sick knowledge that her hope of reprieve had been fulfilled in the way she would least have wanted it to be, she saw her mother bearing down on Meg and Dave, with Linda following at a slower pace; saw Meg and Dave turn startled faces to their approach; and, reluctantly, set off on the line that brought her up to all four of them.

There was no scene. Her mother was the very last person to allow raised voices that would tell the rest of the village the Morrison family's business. Her mother's eyes fixed on the arm Dave had put around Meg's shoulders; then they swept Dave himself, from his dark hair to the polished toes of his Sunday shoes.

"Come here, Meg." For all its quietness the voice she used then still shook with anger. Meg flinched from it, but she didn't move, except to draw closer to Dave. And Dave, although he had flushed under that long look, only tightened his clasp on Meg's shoulder.

"Mrs. Morrison," he said, "it's not what you think. I mean, we're not just—"

"I didn't speak to you, Dave Ferguson."

"I know, but I just wanted to— You see, Mrs. Morrison—" Dave's nerves were getting the better of him— and no wonder, under the stare he had to face. Then quite suddenly, he was calm again, knowing exactly what he wanted to say and saying it with dignity. "Meg and I love one another. We want to get engaged."

It was stupid of him, of course. In their attic room afterwards, when all three of them were discussing it, even Meg had to agree with that. And yet, she argued, Dave didn't know their mother the way they did—the pride that was in her, the determination that they should all "make something of themselves." And in spite of everything she had tried to tell him about it, he had never really grasped what that meant to their mother.

Dave was honest, too. That was why it hadn't occurred to him that the whole thing could have been passed off as just a bit of slap and tickle—which would have made their mother mad enough, certainly, but not so much as the truth had done. Poor gallant Dave, rushing in with the one explanation that had really ruined everything!

"And I had meant it to be so different," Meg told them mournfully. "I was going to work Mam around to the idea of us getting engaged—work her ever so gently around to it. Next year, perhaps, when I'll be finished school, and Dave will be certain of his plans. But now—" Meg's voice went out of control then; and when she had command of it again, she said, "But now I can't do that. Now I might as well reason with a rock, as with Mam. And to think it need never have happened! If you had kept watch for me and Dave, Jinty, the way you promised you always would—if only you had!"

There was no answer to the accusation in Meg's voice, and she didn't try to make one—not even to herself; not even although it was a whole year since the promise had been made, and she had kept it faithfully since then.

But what use was that, now that she finally had let Meg down—with no excuse, either, except curiosity in watching the row between Mr. Elphinston and the Earl, instead of paying attention to her mother as she should have done? And Meg had been so good to her. Always, in spite of the way she could be bossy, too, Meg had been a good, kind sister to her.

She sat in shamed silence remembering Dave's little moment of dignity, with Meg standing by, afraid of the way he had spoken yet still elated by it. And then, as her mother's expression changed from outraged astonishment to scorn, the destruction of that moment.

"Engaged? At the age she is? And to you, of all people! Don't you be impudent to me, boy!"

It had to be heard to be believed, the contempt her mother put into that last word, and it was painful to watch how deep Dave's flush grew as he said,

"I'm not a boy, Mrs. Morrison. I'm nineteen. And I'm a nobody now, I know, but—"

"That's enough. My Meg is a schoolgirl, not yet seventeen. And she'll go on to University, next year. She has a real career ahead of her, boy—"

"I told you, I'm not a boy." Dave was still trying to speak calmly, but the humiliation of it all was beginning to bite deep. And there was worse to come.

"What are you, then? A grease monkey! A garage hand! Is that the kind of fellow that's fit to court a girl with Meg's chances in life? Let me tell you, Dave Ferguson—"

Dave didn't wait to hear what her mother had to tell

149

him. Dave's pride had suffered enough hurt, by that time. He turned on his heel and swung away from them, ignoring the cry Meg sent after him, never even seeing the hand she reached desperately out to him. And then Meg herself was trying to swing away from their mother's reaching hand; Meg shaking with tears and rage, and wildly accusing,

"You wouldn't listen. You wouldn't even listen to him! You just treated him like a kid—a stupid, vulgar kid."

"Because that's exactly what he is. And so are you, it seems—vulgar, if you can't see beyond *his* sort for a husband, and stupid even to be thinking of marrying at the age you are now."

"You're being rotten. You're just being rotten and unfair."

"So that's what I am now? And what have you proved yourself to be? How long have you been meeting that fellow on the sly—eh? How many lies have you told, to manage that for yourself?"

Meg gaped. Meg had been so agitated till then that she had truly forgotten the kind of explaining she would have to do. And what made it worse, was the way their mother went on, not sounding angry now, but just sad and very tired.

"And after all the times I've tried to show you that I'm only strict with you for your own good—so that you could have a career, be somebody, make something of your life."

"But it was because you were so strict," Meg began. "We only kept it secret because—"

"Because you've learned nothing after all, it seems." Remorselessly, their mother took the words away from Meg. "Nothing at all of what I've tried to teach you about the only worthwhile things being the honest ones, the open ones; those that don't need you to be forever keeping secrets, and telling lies to me. Can't you think of the shock that's been to me? Don't you care how you hurt me?"

Meg cared. Of course Meg cared. That was why their mother had had the last word before they all walked home together, in silence, avoiding every opportunity to look at one another. That was why Meg was sitting there now, looking so desperately unhappy.

"What will you do?" Linda asked.

"I love him," Meg said.

Linda clicked her tongue in exasperation. "That wasn't what I asked! And no wonder Mam went on at you. Marrying a village chap and having yards of kids—is that all you can think of?"

"We love each other," Meg said quietly. "They'd be our kids—if we were lucky enough to have any."

There was a long silence. Then Meg got up from where she sat in front of the dressing table, and walked to the window. The cherry tree outside it was a mass of leaves that had turned yellow and were drifting singly downwards to speckle the brown of the earth beneath. With her eyes on the uncertain voyage of one scrap of yellow, Meg said,

"I didn't want to hurt Mam. I don't want to hurt her again."

"You don't have to," Linda told Meg's back. "Once you go up to 'Varsity you'll find there's a lot more fish in the sea than Dave Ferguson. And a lot more interesting things to do, too, than going around with fellows."

Meg didn't answer this. The room became silent again—so silent that it seemed now as if they could almost hear the whisper of the drifting leaves beyond the window.

"What will you do?" Linda's voice repeating her question was loud against the stillness, and very demanding. Meg turned towards it, and they saw that she had been crying. "Well?" Linda asked; and once again Meg answered,

"I love him."

Her voice was steady, in spite of the tears; and this time, although the words were the same, the tone was different. Meg had come to a decision, and she didn't mean to let them know about it yet, but it was still a final one.

12

The winter following that harvest was a green and mild one, and the guests for the shooting parties at the Hall seemed to begin arriving earlier than usual. Every weekend there were groups of them on the local train that connected with the express from London, all of them looking expensive in tweed, and silk, and furs; and all of them, as their luggage was put into the cars the Earl sent to meet them, talking gaily in loud English voices that ignored the presence of everyone except themselves.

"As if we were the dirt beneath their feet," Linda said angrily; and scowled when their mother said she had got herself a job at the Hall for that winter.

"It's just at weekends, to help with the cooking," she explained. "And Mrs. Darnley has another weekend job going, too, if one of you girls should want it."

Mrs. Darnley was the Earl's housekeeper; and Linda scowled again when she heard that the other job was for

153

a kitchen maid. But even if she had wanted that job, she couldn't have taken it because she already had one at weekends, helping Mr. Nelson with the farm accounts. It wasn't possible for Meg either, since she worked all day Saturday, looking after the great gaggle of Nelson kids.

"And that just leaves you, Jinty," her mother said. "But it'll mean late nights every Friday and Saturday, and I doubt you're too young for that."

The chance of getting some money of her own at last was too good to miss. Money meant she would be able to do as Meg and Linda did—buy clothes for herself; so that, at last also, she would have a Sunday dress, instead of being stuck with only her Academy uniform to wear to church.

"I could sleep late on Saturdays and Sundays." She objected, and kept up this argument until her mother agreed,

"I suppose you could. And you'd certainly find Mrs. Darnley easy to get on with. But you'd still have Herr Winkel, the chef, to worry about. He's Swiss, and he's got a wicked temper."

"I won't get in his way," she promised; and eventually her mother decided,

"All right, then. You can try it. But don't blame me if you find it too much for you. It's a long walk to the Hall, remember, and it'll be an even longer one home when you're tired with the night's work."

It was a dark path as well as a long one that led to the Hall—over a mile of walking through woodland; but the Hall itself was a huge place, a great square mansion with hundreds of windows all lit up, and the gleam of those windows guided the final part of their first journey there. On that first night, too, the great double doors of the Hall were open, spilling more light onto the sweep of landscaped gardens in front of it. The lake that formed the centerpiece of the gardens gleamed milky white in the glow from the doorway—"like a moonstone," her mother said, surprising her with the poetry of the remark.

Cars passed them as they followed the gravelled drive that circled the lake—long, opulent, chauffeur-driven cars carrying women who gleamed with jewels, and men in evening dress that made them as stiffly black and white as penguins. There was a discreet flurry of drivers, a glitter of guests, as the cars stopped in front of the Hall; and as they themselves drew level with the doors and the cars were being driven off to be garaged, her mother said,

"Quick! Take a look in before the doors close."

She looked towards the great burst of light that was the chandelier hanging beyond the doorway, blinked to clear her vision of its impact—and there it was, the most famous of all the Hall's features: the long flight of pink marble stairs sweeping up from ground level to the portrait gallery on the floor above. The doors closed, and with her mind still full of the moment's vision, she walked on beside her mother towards the kitchen entrance.

"You saw them?" her mother asked, and she nodded,

but with a question of her own forming in her mind.

There had been a time when Lady Dorothy, the Earl's mistress, had walked all the way down that flight of stairs with nothing but her long golden hair to cover her nakedness. And Lady Dorothy, they said, was slim and beautiful. But that was all something she had heard about when she was really small—too small, even, to know what a mistress was; and so she hadn't been shocked by it. She had liked the picture it made, in fact—Lady Dorothy in her shining cloud of golden hair walking slim and cool and naked-pink down the long flight of cool pink stairs. And she still liked carrying that picture in her mind, even although she did know now how shocking it was. But—

"Was it really true about Lady Dorothy?" she asked.

Her mother looked around, startled, from laying her hand on the latch of the door to the servants' quarters.

"True about what?"

"About her walking down the pink stairs with nothing on?"

"Oh, aye, it was true. The Earl bet her a hundred pounds she wouldn't do that in front of all his house-guests. But she did. And when she got to the foot of the stairs he poured the money, in gold, into her hands. But listen, Jinty—" Her mother let go the latch to take her by the arm. "That was all long ago, before you were born, and you're never to mention it while we're working here. D'you understand? Or any other scandal about the Hall, for that matter of it; or you could get me the sack, as well as yourself. And I need the money from this job, girl. I need it badly."

"It's all right, Mam. I won't talk to anyone," she promised; and with a hand to the latch again, her mother said,

"Good. You'll learn all the faster for that. And this job mightn't be so easy as you think."

"No, Mam." Impatiently she gave the dutiful answer that was always expected of her. The latch clicked. The door opened. She breathed spicy kitchen air, heard pans clattering above the sound of unfamiliar voices, and the next moment found herself among sinks, stoves, racks of gleaming copper pans, and a scatter of strange faces all shrewdly measuring her for the new girl at the Hall.

She was to share a washing-up sink with a fat woman called Kate Wilson, she was told; and was soon aware that Kate had just the kind of scandalous tongue her mother had warned against. That meant trouble from the butler, Mr. Ramenski, who was very loyal to the Earl; and so she was glad of the excuse not to talk much to Kate. Her mother had also been right about the job itself, she discovered, because washing-up at the Hall wasn't just a simple matter of scrubbing pans.

There was bone china to be handled, too, delicate stuff that needed a lot of care; and silver, that had the feel of silk under her fingers. You could tell real silver blindfolded from that silky feel, Mr. Ramenski said; and she liked the idea of that. She liked the big, warm-smelling kitchen, too, and the air of bustling excitement that hung over it. But it all took time to get used to; and when Herr Winkel became really busy with those copper pans, there wasn't any time to spare!

Herr Winkel was as much a tyrant as people said he was, throwing things about the kitchen when he flew into one of his famous rages, and swearing in half a dozen languages—although mostly in German. Yet it was still fascinating to watch the skill and speed of his big, pudgy hands measuring, mixing, chopping. And Herr Winkel could be polite, too, in spite of his temper; a friendly sort of tyrant when something pleased him.

"You are quick, neat," he said, the first time he saw her plucking the pheasants he needed for dinner. "Not like that *Dummkopf* there!" A contemptuous jerk of his head indicated the stolid figure of Kate; and as she had finished work on the birds, he asked, "You like *petits fours,* yes?"

The mere mention of the confections always sent upstairs with the coffee was enough to make her mouth water! "Yes, sir," she told him; and, delightedly, with both hands holding his bulging stomach, he said,

"*Ach, du lieber Gott!* At last, a *Mädchen* who is polite! You shall have some, *mein Liebchen.* You shall have."

On the way home that night, with her mother sharing in the napkinful of *petits fours* he had given her after dinner, she said,

"You're good at making these, Mam; as good as Herr Winkel. And he's always cursing at the time they cost him. Why don't you offer to take them off his hands?"

"Oh, I couldn't speak like that! But—" Her mother's

tone altered, became oddly uncertain. "Do you—d'you really think I should?"

"'Course I do." She was becoming bold on these homeward walks, with darkness to cover her and the knowledge of a shared experience making her feel that, at last, she was on a level footing with her mother. "I'll tell him, if you don't like to say it. I'm not scared of him."

"No. No, there'll be no need." Her mother was suddenly brisk again, as decisive as ever; and by the time of their next weekend at the Hall, the change had been made. Herr Winkel handed over the vegetable preparation to Kate Wilson, while her mother was set to work on the fondant and crystallized fruit for the *petits fours*. But just for the moment, it looked as if there might be trouble over this.

"Favoritism, that's what it is," Kate said sourly. "You Morrisons are a pair of stuck-up bitches, if you ask me."

Herr Winkel wasn't around then, and it was Mr. Ramenski who came to her mother's rescue. "Nobody ask you, stupid!" he said sharply. "But you are still wrong. For the *pâtisserie*, Mrs. Morrison has craft certificate."

Mr. Ramenski's English wasn't too good, but he could always make himself clear enough to let Kate see he wouldn't stand any nonsense from her. Kate went off, muttering under her breath about "the dirty Russki"— which was simply spite, of course, because Mr. Ramenski couldn't help being a Russian and he certainly wasn't dirty the way Kate meant it. Mr. Ramenski had very good manners, and he never pawed the maids the way the footmen on his staff were always trying to do.

"You never told me about any craft certificate," she challenged her mother on that night's walk home. "How did you learn? Where did you get this certificate?"

"From Brodie's, in Edinburgh."

"*The* Brodie's? The big bakery firm?"

"M'phm. My father knew the Brodie family. And like I've told you all so often, in my day, an education wasn't supposed to be important for girls. But my father thought I should at least learn a craft; and after he spoke to Mr. John Brodie for me, I was allowed to serve an apprenticeship with the firm."

"But I always thought you were a nurse before you married."

"That was after my time at Brodie's. Sugar was rationed during the War, and that's when I took up nursing."

"You never said anything about that before, either."

"Well, I don't have to tell you everything about myself, do I?"

Something she had never thought of before occurred to her then. Her mother had lived a whole life before she herself had been born! And there were so many things she didn't know about that life that her mother was really a stranger to her. Curiosity to discover this stranger immediately overcame her, prompting one question after another.

"Did you like nursing? Were you good at it?"

"I did it well enough. And yes, I liked it—especially

when I worked at the military hospital. The soldiers there were a cheery lot, in spite of the way some of them were smashed up."

"And was that how you met Dad?"

"No, that was how I met—" Abruptly her mother checked the word—or was it a name?—on her lips; and it was a moment or so before she ventured to ask,

"Who did you meet?"

"The man I fell in love with. He—We were to have been married, but he was killed in the War."

Another silence, respectful on her part this time, before her curiosity forced the next venture. "And this man—was it really bad when he died? Did your heart break?"

"Hearts don't break. That's poet's language. You should read less of romantic rubbish, Jinty, and more of decent books."

"All right, then. How did it feel?"

"Pretty bad. It was—oh, as if there was a high wall between everyone else and me, and I was crouching down on my own side of the wall just wanting to die too."

Pity for the desolation in the picture her mother had drawn, moved sharply within her. The feeling was too much to bear, and hastily she created something to banish it.

"But then you did meet Dad. And it wasn't so terrible then, was it?"

"You're full of questions tonight, aren't you? What're you poking and prying around for?"

"I'm not, Mam." It was reassurance she wanted now; the happy-ending sort of reassurance that meant she wouldn't be haunted by the thought of the lonely figure crouching down in pain behind that dividing wall. "I just want to hear the proper end of it; you know—about you falling in love with Dad."

"I didn't. He fell in love with me."

"But you married him!"

"It's not necessarily the same thing."

"But—Didn't you come to love him? Don't you love him now?"

"Yes, I did. And yes, I do. He was so kind. And that was one time when I really needed kindness. Besides—" Her mother hesitated, as if cautioning herself; and then went on, "He loved me so much he was willing to make all my problems his own. And the way things were then, that meant a lot to me."

They were at the very darkest stretch of the path by then; the stretch where they had to link arms to avoid bumping into one another. She had been shy of this at first, because they weren't the sort of family that went in for such seemingly affectionate gestures; but now, as she realized how her mother had begun to tremble, she was glad of their closeness. She hugged the arm under her own a little more tightly, and said,

"I'm glad it worked out all right."

Unexpectedly, her mother laughed, and told her, "You're taking yourself as the proof of that, I suppose."

The answering hug that went with the remark made her mother and the stranger seem one person again; but there were still things she wanted to know before she could accept this idea.

"Would it have been different for you," she asked, "if you'd married that other man—the one who died? I mean, was he poor like Dad, or was he well-off?"

"He had money. He came of good family. Yes, it would have been different. I could still have made something of myself."

"Like you could have done if you'd had the educational chances we have?"

"Isn't that why I keep trying to impress all three of you with the importance of making careers for yourselves? I don't want to see you girls suffering my regrets, repeating my mistakes."

"But you couldn't help the way things were with you."

"Not all of it. But some of it could have been different, if only I'd had sense at the time. Or if I'd had the guidance I'm prepared to give you girls."

They walked in silence for a few moments, still physically close, and with herself feeling that there was now also a different kind of intimacy between them. The feeling strengthened until it gave her the confidence to say,

"I suppose that's why you're so hard on Meg. Because you really are, Mam; harder than you are with Linda and me."

"That's nonsense. But even if it were true, Meg's reckless. She could do herself harm."

"I know. But it wouldn't be like that if you let her

see Dave again. She really does love him, Mam. Like you said you loved—"

"Hold your tongue, girl! You don't know what you're talking about."

Suddenly they were back on the old footing, with her mother snatching her arm away, and herself being treated like a child again. The disappointment, at first, was sharp. But, she reasoned, the winter wasn't past yet. There would be a lot more of homeward walks in the dark; and so there was bound to be a lot more also of moments when her mother forgot to lecture, and the two of them could be just like people talking to one another. She began looking forward to this; and then was dismayed to find that the winter wasn't past yet, either, so far as the nature of her duties at the Hall was concerned.

She was to start helping with the work upstairs, Mrs. Darnley told her. The between-maid had given notice. Mr. Ramenski was short of footmen, and they needed someone to collect the glasses and coffee cups that guests would persist in leaving littered about in odd places after the main clearing-up was done.

"Someone with a neat appearance, Jinty," Mrs. Darnley said, producing a frilly cap and apron to wear with her kitchen maid's dress of plain, dark blue. "And that means you."

"But I've never been upstairs!" With dismay turning to panic at the thought of the uncharted mysteries beyond the green baize of the kitchen door, she protested against the arrangement. "I won't know where to go."

"I show you," Mr. Ramenski told her. His dark, slightly almond-shaped eyes looked her up and down. "You look good; pretty. And you are smart to learn. Come."

She followed him through the green door and into a maze of carpeted corridors, listening intently as he threw open doors to name one room after another. The library, the gun room, the west sitting room, the ballroom—he was very careful in explaining the plan of all the ones she would need to know. She filed the information neatly in her mind, watching the gleam of his smooth dark head moving steadily along in front of her, and beginning to wonder about the man himself.

He was a White Russian, Mrs. Darnley said. That meant he had fought against the Red Revolution in his own country, and so he would never be able to go back there. But did he really want to go back? The Earl had also been in that fighting, and Mrs. Darnley said there had been one time when he had saved Mr. Ramenski's life from the Reds. That was why Mr. Ramenski was always so loyal to him. And so maybe—

"Come!" His voice startled her out of her speculations. "I show you where you collect glasses from the balcony above the ballroom."

They climbed broad, shallow stairs, and came out onto a railed balcony overlooking the ballroom on all four sides. A tall, gray-haired woman came towards them from the far side of the balcony. She was slim, graceful in a long, silky robe trailing and floating behind her, and she had once been beautiful.

"Ramenski—" she began, and then checked herself to ask, "Who's this, Ramenski?"

"Village girl," Mr. Ramenski explained, "to help upstairs sometimes, for the winter."

"H'mm. Well, she looks clean. Is she honest?"

It was an extraordinary feeling to be standing there hearing herself talked about as if she were a thing, instead of a person. It made her understand how Linda felt. She waited while Mr. Ramenski gravely answered the questions, wondering who the woman was; and was startled when he addressed her as "Lady Dorothy."

Gray hair . . . But Lady Dorothy was golden-haired! Her dream of the pink and gold figure stepping lightly down the long pink stairs, collapsed into ruins. The knowledge of passing time touched her like a cold hand laid on her heart; and as the ravaged face of Lady Dorothy turned towards her, she felt a great compassion for it.

"Ramenski," Lady Dorothy said sharply, "tell her she must learn not to stare. Otherwise, she'll do. And Ramenski, I've been looking for you to let you know. He's drinking again."

"If I may suggest, m'lady—*pas devant la bonne.*"

The two of them drifted a few steps from her. A murmur of conversation in French came from them. At one point in the conversation, she noted, Mr. Ramenski took Lady Dorothy's hands in his own and pressed them, as if giving some sort of reassurance. Then it was over. Lady Dorothy was passing her in a long trail of silken robe, and Mr. Ramenski was beckoning her on along the balcony.

"Here," he said; and with the gesture he made she took in the fact that the balcony held a number of small, gilded tables and more of the red and gilt chairs she had seen arranged around the ballroom floor. "Wine glasses, coffee cups, ashtrays—sometimes you must collect from these tables. But not to disturb the guests, you understand. Always, here and in other places, you must be very quiet, like a mouse. Yes?"

"Yes," she repeated. "Yes, Mr. Ramenski."

"Good. I leave you. You find your own way back to kitchen."

That wasn't nearly such a puzzle as she'd thought it would be. And she'd enjoyed being upstairs, after all, in spite of her fear of it! There was to be even more of interest in that winter than she'd hoped for, she thought, and once again began looking forward.

13

It wasn't until all the guests had gone in to dinner that she was ever needed upstairs, and so there wasn't much chance of her encountering any of them in the rooms that had to be checked for dirty glasses. She was quick about it, all the same. Always, too, as Mr. Ramenski had told her, she was "quiet like a mouse"—just in case she might run into someone who would notice she wasn't a real between-maid; and it was only on the balcony above the ballroom that she found herself tempted to linger.

That was after dinner, of course, when they had the dancing; and only then if there were no guests around when she went up there. But once she'd made sure of that, and if she was careful not to be noticed from the ballroom itself, she could look down for a while at the dancing; and what she managed to see of it like this was so unbelievably exotic to her she never could resist that temptation.

For a start, there was a real dance band, not just ordinary chaps with fiddles and accordions like they had in the village. These were proper musicians in white jackets, with trombones and saxophones, just like she had seen in films. Then there were the footmen, standing still as posts in their livery of red and white; the dancers themselves, gliding in a graceful, gleaming swirl under the gleam of the huge chandelier that lit the place; and finally there was the Earl. He was always resplendent with the blue sash and gold star of some sort of Order across the starched white of his shirtfront; always—even when Lord Garvald and Lady Dorothy were there—quite clearly the center of things. But he didn't dance, she noticed; not when she was watching at least: and this gave him an air of aloofness from the others—almost, it finally struck her, as if he had created this grand function only to lose interest in it after all.

That, it seemed to her then, was a terrible waste; and not just a waste of power and money, either. There was something sad about it, too, something lonely, she thought; and then was astonished to realize what the thought meant. She used to be so scared of the Earl, and yet here she was, actually feeling sorry for him! And what would *he* make of that—a kitchen maid peering down from the balcony and feeling sorry for the Earl?

The thought of all this kept recurring to her, but she mentioned nothing of it to anyone until she looked up from the balcony railing one night and saw a pair of dark, almond-shaped eyes fixed on her. Mr. Ramenski was watching her from the other side of the balcony. In a flurry of guilt, then, she turned to pick up her tray; but Mr. Ramenski didn't seem to be annoyed with her. He even helped her to clear up the glasses on the balcony tables, and this finally made her bold enough to say,

"The Earl never seems to join in the dancing, Mr. Ramenski."

He shrugged. "No. Dancing is all past for him."

"Then he used to dance?" She looked up from her tray with the question, and was surprised to see Mr. Ramenski's expression—a half smile, with a gleam of remembering in his eyes.

"Oh yes, indeed—wild, like a Cossack. At parties here, you understand." The smiling expression faded; and, sighing, Mr. Ramenski added under his breath, "Such parties!"

They went downstairs together to the butler's pantry; and there, still encouraged by the feeling that she was not out of favor after all, she ventured another question.

"Mr. Ramenski, why did the Earl go to Russia to fight against the Red Revolution? It wasn't his war, after all, like it was yours; and he never even touches a gun here."

Mr. Ramenski looked really startled for a moment. Then, quickly, he said, "Don't ask, *babushka*. You mustn't ask this. Is not for you to know."

She flushed scarlet with embarrassment at her blunder, and mumbled an apology.

"Okay, okay," Mr. Ramenski told her. "But you don't talk more about it—not to me, not to anyone, huh?"

"Oh no, Mr. Ramenski!" She was so vehement in her assurance that he smiled. The smile changed to a long, serious look, then he said,

"Listen, you are sensible girl. You don't chatter. You do something for me?" She nodded, and he went on, "You clear glasses from the library. Right? Okay. If the Earl is there late, when you clear up, you slip the word to me, eh? But only if he is on his own there, of course. And never do you tell anyone I ask you to do this. You understand?"

He wasn't going to give her his reason for asking, she realized; but she could guess at it, of course. Sometimes when she went late at night and quiet like a mouse to clear empty glasses from the library, the Earl was sitting there alone in front of the fire with a decanter of whisky on the low table beside his chair. And Lady Dorothy had told Mr. Ramenski, *"He's drinking again."* But Mr. Ramenski had given that reassuring squeeze on Lady Dorothy's hands; and very likely he was using anyone he could trust—including herself now—to help him guess the moment when he would have to persuade the Earl to leave his whisky and go to bed.

"I'll do that, Mr. Ramenski," she promised. "I'll slip you the word."

The serious expression lifted from Mr. Ramenski's face. His dark eyes gleamed approvingly; and the next time she went late into the library, she was quieter about it than ever. The Earl was there, but all she could see of him was a fraction of his face jutting beyond the high side-wings of his armchair and a pair of long, black-trousered legs stretched out to the fire. The decanter of whisky stood, as usual, on the table beside the chair, and it was two-thirds empty. Tiptoeing, she retreated to find Mr. Ramenski and tell him of this. On yet another occasion, the same thing happened; but on the third occasion she found the Earl alone late with his whisky decanter, things turned out differently.

There was a big, shallow bowl full of snowdrops on the table beside the decanter that night. They reminded her of the snowdrops at Toby's funeral, and every so often as she moved noiselessly around the library, she found herself pausing to look at them. That made her slow in collecting the used glasses, and a little careless with them. Two of them rattled against one another in her hand. There was a movement of the long black legs, and from the depths of the armchair a voice called,

"You, there! Come where I can see you."

She stood for a moment, trembling, then went unwillingly towards the chair. She faced the Earl across the small table with the whisky and the snowdrops on it, and tried to control the movement of her hands smoothing nervously at the front of her apron.

"I'm not stupid, you know. I can put two and two together. Maid slips in, maid slips out—very quietly, pretending she's never been there at all. Five minutes later the faithful Ramenski appears and starts persuading his lordship it's time to go to bed. Why d'you do it, eh? Spying on me!"

His voice was harsh. His eyes peering up at her from

under shaggy eyebrows, had a blurred, hostile look. She swallowed hard to dispel the traces of her old fear rising in her throat, and said as best she could,

"I have to do what I'm told, sir."

"I'm not a 'sir.' I'm a lord, an earl. 'M'lord'—that's what you call me."

"I know, sir—m'lord. I'm sorry."

He blinked at her, as if trying to focus his blurry stare, and said wearily, "That's all right. Rude of me to tell you that. Shouldn't be rude to servants, goddammit. Very bad form."

His eyes were focussing now: He was beginning to see her face properly, she guessed, and wasn't surprised when he exclaimed,

"Hey, I know you! Kid who was scared in the woods, aren't you?" She nodded, and he went on, "That's right. Never forget a face. Good attribute for a feudal lord to have, don't you know."

He was mocking himself with that last remark, she realized, but there was nothing she could do except let him ramble on. "Morrison, Morrison . . ." he recalled her name from the depths of memory, and added triumphantly, "Jinty—the smallest one. Right? The kid in Miss Carson's class. The one who brought the—"

He caught himself up there, his eyes going to the bowl of snowdrops. She waited for him to look at her again; and when he did, it was to say quietly—almost humbly, she thought,

"I'm sorry. I shouldn't have reminded you."

173

"No," she agreed, not knowing any way of dissembling the truth; which was that it still hurt to think of Toby. He stared at her and said,

"That's straight from the shoulder. Haven't you ever heard of white lies—the kind that save people's feelings?"

"Yes," she admitted, "but I couldn't think of one. And anyway—" She hesitated, uncertain of how to put her thought, and then finished awkwardly, "I don't like to tell lies about things that matter to me."

He was still staring; but finally he reached out to the decanter and refilled his glass from it. He sipped the whisky; and then, with his eyes coming back to her over the rim of the glass, he muttered,

"Whole goddam houseful of guests, and I wind up at night talking to a kitchen maid!"

A sense that this was unjust to both of them drove her to say, "I'm not really a kitchen maid. This is just a winter weekend job for me. I'm at the Academy, and my Mam says she'll send me to University if I'm good enough."

"Then you'd better be good enough," he told her. "She's had a hard life, your mother. I know that. My God, I remember her in the War, when young Roger Belaney was killed. She—"

He stopped abruptly, the glass poised halfway to his lips. "You don't know what I'm talking about, do you."

It was a statement, rather than a question; and once again she was left not knowing how to answer, because her mind had leapt immediately from the name "Roger

Belaney" to her mother's young man who had been killed in the War. But that was her mother's business, wasn't it? And there wouldn't be any more confidences on the road home if she spoke about it to anyone else. She looked dumbly at the Earl for a moment or two, then shook her head and asked timidly,

"May I go now, please?"

He took another sip of his drink, waved the glass at her and said, "Yes, yes. Off you go and tell Ramenski his lordship's boozing away his sorrows again."

She scuttled back to her trayful of glasses, and was going out with them when he called, "But listen. Make more noise the next time you come in. I don't want to have to strain my ears for Ramenski's spies. And talk to me again, d'you hear? I'm not an ogre, goddammit!"

The Earl's language was shocking sometimes, although he was polite enough in other ways. She told Mr. Ramenski something of the encounter; but only something, because the snowdrops and the man who was killed were private to herself and her mother. Mr. Ramenski pondered what she said, pursing his lips and frowning over the thought of letting her break the rule that said upstairs staff could speak only when they had to acknowledge an order or answer a question; but finally he decided,

"Yes. Silence is not good for him. If this is what he wants, you speak."

But what could she say, apart from "Good evening"? On the first occasion after that, when she found him alone in the library, she ventured the greeting, and got only a grunt in reply. But the next time was different.

"Come here," he told her; and again she went to stand where he could see her.

"I've been talking to Archie Meikle about you," he said. "He says you're fey. Are you?"

"Yes, sir—m'lord," she told him. "At least, I think I am."

"But you don't like that feeling, do you?"

She stood trying to decide just what it was like for her to be gripped by the foreboding sense she had learned to recognize as "fey." "No," she said finally, "I don't like it. It frightens me, makes me sort of uneasy. And yet, it attracts me, too. That's the odd thing about it. But there's nothing I can do about that, is there? I mean, it's not something I can run away from."

"No. No, you can't." He sat silent, staring into his glass, then shot a sudden upward look at her and said, "Meikle also says you're fey about me. Is that true?"

The knights in the churchyard . . .

"That was something that happened long ago when I was small—only eleven years old." She was speaking defensively now, afraid of the challenge in his voice. "I— It was when I used to be scared of you."

"Like you were in the woods, eh? But you're not scared now, are you?"

He was still the Earl, all-mighty master of the Hall and of the huge Ballinford Estate. But he was also the bleak, grieving figure at the graveside, the jovial conspirator at the prize-giving, the tower of triumph in the barley field, the champion of corn dolly against Mr.

Elphinston. And added to that now, he was just a lonely man with a houseful of guests he wasn't interested in; an old man brooding over the Ballinford doom—and his own powerlessness to save Lord Garvald from it? The vast stretches of the library beyond the circle of fire-light seemed to throng suddenly with the ghostly figures of all the eldest sons who had died untimely deaths; and the fey feeling was strong in her as she said,

"No, not now. I'm scared *for* you now."

He looked at her face, intently, reading the expression on it. Then he nodded, and said, "Yes. You'll know. You'll know when it's going to happen."

She didn't understand that, any more than she had understood the reason for her own remark; and when he had lowered his eyes to sit staring into his glass again, she slipped quietly away from the library. He always answered her after that, when she said "Good evening" to him, and sometimes that was all he said. But there were other times when he talked to her—seriously on occasion, asking her about herself and her family, and teasingly also when it suited him, making a joke of the careful way she did her job. But never again did he speak of her being fey, and never once did he mention the Ballinford doom or anything connected with it.

Mr. Ramenski was pleased with her. "You are good for him," he said; and she wondered what possible dif-ference it could make to the Earl to talk occasionally and for only a few minutes at a time to a kitchen maid. Mrs. Darnley was pleased because Mr. Ramenski was pleased. Herr Winkel had good words for her, too, because she didn't neglect her work in the kitchen for the work upstairs. She was in high favor all around, in fact; and as they walked home together from their last night at the Hall, her mother said approvingly,

"You'll have a career yet, Jinty. This job has taught you discipline, you see; and that's something you must learn if you're ever going to be able to apply yourself to anything worthwhile."

She thought of the thousands of dishes she had washed since the winter began, and said ruefully, "It's taught me the real cost of a new dress!"

They both laughed at that. They had laughed quite a lot by this time on these walks home, sauntering arm in arm at a pace that allowed for the weariness they felt then, and retelling one another the experiences of the evening. There had been plenty of these, too, because evenings in the Hall kitchen always seemed to move from crisis to crisis; and although they could never be sure if it was Herr Winkel's temper that produced each crisis, or whether it was the crisis that caused the temper, either way it still seemed funny to them.

"It was the same under M'sieu Favager at Brodie's," her mother recalled. "I was the same age you were at the beginning of this winter, when I started there—thirteen and a few months. But I didn't take any harm from it, and that's what really decided me to let you try the job."

"Did you look like me then?"

"Oh yes. Skinny, and dark. But my hair was long, of

course. It was the great thing in those days to grow your hair long enough to sit on—"

Naked-pink sylph in the cloud of golden hair stepping slowly down the long pink stairs . . . The vanished picture flickered briefly again across her mind; but her mother was still talking, her words building up a different sort of picture.

"—and so there I was my first morning in Brodie's, hair in pigtails because I was still too young to wear it up, elastic-sided boots that squeaked—"

She listened intently as her mother went on talking about Brodie's and M'sieu Favager, about learning to make fondant and pull sugar, about the day she was finally allowed to put her hair up and was no longer the youngest apprentice. The picture of the thin dark girl steadily and quietly applying herself to learning a craft grew ever clearer in her mind. The woman she knew and the girl she had been imagining began merging again into one person; but, like it had been before, there was still something she had to ask before this could happen properly. She waited until her mother seemed to have no more to say about Brodie's, then put her question.

"And how old were you when you fell in love with Roger Belaney?"

She had meant to say "the soldier," but the name just slipped out the way that sort of thing always seemed to happen with her when she was deep in thought. The arm holding her own tightened convulsively, pulling them both to a sudden halt. Roughly, gaspingly, her mother demanded,

"Where did you hear that name?"

She hedged, remembering Mr. Ramenski's instructions, and the reason for them. "The Earl. He talked to me one night when I was clearing glasses from the library."

"Talked to you? About what? What did he say?"

"Nothing much. Just told me to do well at school because you'd had a hard life, and that he remembered you in the War when this Roger Belaney was killed."

"Was that all? Are you sure that was all?"

"Quite sure, Mam. That really was all."

"And did he ever mention that name to you again?"

"No, never."

"Then how did you know it was—it was *his* name? The man I told you about."

"I didn't. I just supposed it was."

Her mother sighed. The tight grip slackened and they walked on again in silence until, cautiously, she asked,

"How did the Earl know about him, Mam?"

"The Earl was Colonel of his regiment. And don't ask any more questions. I don't want to talk about it. And you're not to mention it again, either. Do you hear? You're not to speak about it to anyone, ever again."

Was that the real reason for the Earl giving her father a job—because he had felt so sorry for her mother when Belaney was killed? Hurriedly, because she was so dismayed by her mother's peremptory tone, she dismissed

180

this last question from her mind, and tried to repair the breach her indiscretion had opened.

"Don't worry, Mam. I truly won't ever mention it. And I don't want to speak of it now, either. I'd much rather talk about the money we've earned, and what we're going to do with it. You know?"

It was a favorite subject with them, spending their money in advance, but now her mother said brusquely,

"We've done that over and over again."

"I know, Mam. But tell me just one more time what you're going to do with yours."

"No," her mother said. "If we must talk like that, tell me about the dress you're going to buy. Try to make up your mind about it."

"I can't," she protested. "You know I never can. It's a different one every time I try to imagine it. You tell me about the house, Mam. Go on. I like to hear you say it."

Redecorating the house—that was the dream her mother had confided in her. The place had become like a prison to her, she had said, always with the same walls, the same colors; and, year by year, everything getting shabbier and duller. That was why she had needed the money so badly. She had to have it if she was ever going to break that prison feeling with new curtains, new paint, new wallpaper. . . .

"Well—" Her mother started reluctantly, and then gradually became caught up again in the dream. The woodwork of their house began to gleam white. The walls were stripped of old paper. The old curtains were thrown in the bucket. New paper appeared. "Pale blue, with a gold line in it," her mother said. Curtains patterned in light and dark blue were hung at the windows. "And cherry-red," her mother added. "That's what I'm going to have for the cushion covers and the hearth rug. Cherry-red against the pale blue. That's what I've always wanted, and that's what I'm going to have; a pale background with big blobs of bright color."

She was talking fast now and the final words were a tongue twister. She stumbled over them, repeated them slowly, and then the two of them took the whole phrase up like a chant keeping time to their steps, slapping their feet hard down on the path and giggling at themselves for doing so. Coming out of the woods they walked more sedately, and were as quiet as usual when they let themselves into the house. The light was on in the living room, and her mother said,

"Linda's still up."

That was also part of the usual pattern; Meg and her father in bed, Linda still awake and sitting by the fire studying a textbook on Accountancy; and when they came in that night with the flush of enjoyment still on their faces, Linda looked curiously at them.

"I'll make some tea," her mother said; and disappeared into the kitchen.

She moved to the table and began stacking the books Meg had left lying there. Come the spring, Meg was due to sit the Higher exams that would give her entrance to University, and she was studying hard for that. But Meg was untidy—not like Linda, with her books always neatly arranged beside her chair at the fire.

"You look pleased with yourself," Linda told her.

There had been another night when they'd come in with that same flush on their faces, and Linda had said then, *Being a kitchen maid seems to suit our Jinty.* There had been obvious sarcasm, too, in the tone of that remark; and so now, she simply nodded, not sure what answers to give.

"Been spending your money ahead of time again?" Linda went on. "Is that it?"

She gave another nod; and then, because her mind was so full of it, found that she simply couldn't help confessing,

"But I still don't know what kind of dress to buy. It's too difficult. I can't make up my mind about it."

Linda stood up, closing her book. "No problem," she said. "I'll help you."

"Will you? Will you really?" With Linda's flair for clothes to help her, the dress was bound to be a success, and she stood there with her eyes open and her mouth open, quite unable to believe her luck.

"Why not?" Linda smiled at her, baiting the trap. "You can do a favor for me in return, can't you?"

And then, like a fool she had walked straight into the trap, promising Linda, "Oh yes, of course. Anything at all, Linda. Anything!"

14

Linda and she had a marvelous time shopping together in Haimston.

"It's spring now; time for a fresh, light color," Linda said. "Pale green—that would be 'you,' I think. And with that narrow waist, a flared skirt would look well."

"And it's fashionable—" Eagerly she began offering her own contribution, but Linda cut her short.

"That's not important. What *is* important is learning to take out of fashion only what suits your own figure and your own coloring. Now! How much cash do you have?"

She had worked for fifteen weeks at eight shillings a week. "H'mm," Linda said. "Six pounds. Well, look, Jinty. For that, if we're careful, we can get you shoes and a handbag, too. What's more, if you bought a suit, rather than a dress, you'd have a whole outfit. And then you needn't spoil the effect by having to wear your school coat over it."

It all sounded too good to be true, but Linda seemed to know exactly how to make it come true. Linda knew just which rail of clothes to go to in every shop they tried. Linda knew all about materials, and styles, and sizes. The figure posing and pirouetting before the mirror in the green suit that Linda eventually chose, didn't seem to be herself at all, but someone taller, older, more graceful.

"But you have to try it with the shoes," Linda told her. "And you should choose a background color for those—something that'll go with the next thing you buy, as well as with this."

She wasn't sure how to name the color of the shoes—deep cream, or pale tan; but it was a background color, all right. She could have worn them with anything. And the handbag exactly matched them.

"Always wear matched leather," Linda instructed her. "It's smarter, and so it looks expensive, even if it isn't. And you've got good legs. Those shoes show them off well."

The shoes had inch and a half heels. She'd never worn anything but flat-heeled school shoes before then, and the girl in green was so much more graceful in these that the next sight of her in the mirror left her speechless with pleasure.

"Here." Linda came across the shop carrying a creamy-tan-colored straw hat. "It's your size, and you've got enough left to buy it. Try it with the suit."

She hadn't considered buying a hat, and she was tempted. But she had plans for the money that was left;

and so she turned away before the temptation grew too much for her.

"I want to buy something for Mam," she said. "Some perfume."

"But Mam's got her own money. And she earned more than you did."

"I know. But she's not spending any of it on herself. And she likes perfume."

"Oh well." Linda sounded disgusted. "If you want to spoil everything by being noble—"

But it wasn't spoiled. On the bus home, with her lap full of parcels and the bottle of perfume making a hard knob in her pocket, she was sure of that. She was still the girl in the new suit who looked nearer sixteen than thirteen, and nothing could take that away from her. They got out of the bus; and Linda sprang the trap on her.

"About the favor you said you'd do for me," she said casually. "There's nothing much to it. I just want to speak to the Earl, that's all. About a job."

"But it's Mrs. Darnley you have to see, if you want a job."

"It's not that kind of a job. *And* I'm not going into the Hall by the kitchen quarters. I'm going in by the front door, and I want you to fix that for me."

"But Linda—!" She was appalled at the idea. "I can't do that!"

"Of course you can," Linda said impatiently. "I've heard Mam talk. I know how pally you are with that butler fellow, Ramenski. And you said you'd do anything for me."

There was no use in arguing. Linda had the one unanswerable retort to every argument—"*You gave your word.*" But she persisted, all the same; and a week later, when they were walking together to the Hall, she was still arguing. Linda hadn't wanted her to be there, either, and she was still having to insist that Mr. Ramenski had said she must come.

"For *bona fides*, you understand," he had told her when she had eventually summoned the courage to make the request of him, and he had got over his own astonishment at it. "I do this thing for you, Jinty, because you have worked well. But you must be guarantee for your sister that she does not come to the Hall to be grand for herself, and waste the Earl's time."

His melancholy Slav eyes took them in at the door—herself in her usual school dress, Linda in the gray suit that looked as casually elegant as all her clothes. But there was no time for them to admire the pink marble staircase, no chance for her to discover how Linda was affected by a first sight of such a marvel. Mr. Ramenski's glance had been swift. Now he was stalking too quickly ahead of them for conversation to be possible; and her own heart was thudding too madly, in any case, for her to be really concerned with what Linda was thinking.

"The Misses Morrison, my lord."

Mr. Ramenski announced them from the door of the library, as expressionless as if it were an everyday thing for him to usher in two village girls to visit the Earl. The heavy door closed noiselessly behind his retreat from the library, and the Earl turned towards them. Standing, with his back to the fire, he looked them both up and down; then his gaze came to rest on Linda.

"Well?" His voice was quiet but there was a formidable hint of challenge in it. She looked at Linda, praying that Mr. Ramenski had been wrong about the prospect of his time being wasted. Linda spoke, sounding perfectly cool and self-possessed.

"I want a job, m'lord. And you can help me. I've thought it all out, and if you care to listen—" She paused inviting interruption with a look; but when the Earl simply nodded, she went on,

"I've always done well at school; and next year, instead of the term exams in May, I could be doing the same as my sister Meg will be doing this year— sitting the Higher exams I'd need to pass before going on to University. But that doesn't appeal to me, because I don't want to spend the better part of another eighteen months in the village. I want to get out of it as fast as I know how, and the only way to do that is through a job."

"What sort of a job?" Linda's smooth flow of talk had intrigued the Earl, and there was interest in his voice now. "As I recall, you must be around—let me see—sixteen? And that's not old enough to earn a wage that'll allow you to live away from home."

"I was sixteen in January this year," Linda told him. "But I said I'd thought it all out. I know very well I'll need something that gives me bed and board until I'm old enough to keep myself; and so that leaves me two choices—a hospital, or a hotel. But I don't want to nurse—and anyway, there's no good hospital will take student nurses at sixteen."

"You won't get a hotel job at that age either," the Earl told her. "Not on the administrative side, at least. And that, I take it, is where you would want to be?"

"Exactly!" Linda agreed. "And I think I'd do well there, too. Look—here's my latest school report card." Deftly she opened her handbag and took her Academy report card from it. "There." Pointing, as she handed it to the Earl, she added, "You'll see my passes in English, French, Latin, Geography, and Maths. They're all high— the highest in my year. And you'll see there, too, that Maths is my best subject; which means I'd be an asset in a hotel office."

"Maths isn't Accountancy," the Earl started, "and if you were working on hotel bookkeeping—"

"M'lord." Coolly Linda broke into his objection. "I've pulled order out of the Ballinford Mains Farm accounts, haven't I?"

"You did that?" The Earl glanced up from studying the card, his face startled; and nodding, she said,

"That's how I spent every Saturday this winter—as you can check with Mr. Gillan and Mr. Nelson, if you want to."

"But for heaven's sake, girl!" The Earl was really thrown out of his stride now. "Why hotel work? You could do better than that, it seems to me."

"But not to me," Linda said calmly. "I can rise up the ladder in a hotel, the same as I could anywhere. I want to travel. I'll keep studying to improve my French, and once I've mastered the routine work, I'll be able to take a job in any country I choose. Meanwhile, I'll live well. I'll meet people—people with money, and mix with them—"

"Not if you're staff, you won't," the Earl interrupted; but Linda simply smiled, and said,

"I won't make the mistake of mixing in the hotel where I happen to be working. And I think I know enough about dress to let me pass for a guest in any other."

The Earl looked her up and down. She stood calmly accepting his survey; and, with the confidence of the smile still on her face beginning to draw an answering smile from him, he handed back the report card.

"You're a cool one, aren't you?" he remarked, watching her return it to her handbag. "But you haven't yet said how I come into all this."

"I thought you'd have guessed," Linda told him. "You're Chairman of the Board of Forsyth International Hotels, after all."

"I see." The Earl nodded. "You couldn't fail to get a job in Forsyth Hotels—not if you produced a reference from the Chairman of the Board. Is that it?"

"Only if you agree with my own opinion that I'd be an asset to the firm," Linda said primly. "That's why I wanted to speak face to face with you, like this; so that you could judge."

"H'mm." The Earl fingered his chin, considering his next move, and then asked, "I take it that all this has your parents' consent?"

"Of course." Linda didn't bat an eyelid as she uttered the lie—*and how could she have interfered at that moment? How could she possibly have out-argued that glib tongue and proved Linda was lying?*

"In that case," the Earl said, and he was grinning openly now, "my judgment is that you are a young lady of extraordinary initiative and determination; so much so, that I shouldn't be surprised if you finished up in *my* place on the Board!"

For the first time then, Linda looked a bit embarrassed. She coughed behind her hand, glanced down at her handbag, and looked up again to say,

"Then you'll give me the reference?"

"Willingly." The Earl turned towards the little writing desk at one side of the fireplace. For a minute, he bent over it, his big form almost hiding it from their view. Then he straightened, and turned to Linda with a sheet of thick, smooth notepaper in one extended hand.

"There you are, Miss Morrison."

Three lines of big, scrawly writing stood out below the golden crest heavily embossed at the head of the paper. *To the Managers of Forsyth International Hotels. The services of Miss Linda Morrison will be a considerable asset to the Company. I wholeheartedly recommend her employment.* Those, and the signature *Ballinford*, were all that the paper held. Linda's fingers closed on it. Linda, with her face lit up suddenly in smiling excitement, began making a formal speech of thanks; but the Earl cut her short, with a nod and one uplifted hand.

"You can thank me by making good use of it," he said; and looking him straight in the eye, Linda promised,

"I shall. Believe me, I shall!"

The next moment they were both outside the library again, and she was turning on Linda, furiously accusing,

"You're a liar! A rotten liar. You never asked permission."

"So what if I didn't?" Linda didn't even bother to look up from her gloating over the sheet of crested paper. "There's no need to be so excited about that. This is only a second string, you ninny. A standby, that's all."

"A standby? What're you *talking* about?"

"About Mam, and the fact that she's determined I'll be a Chartered Accountant. But Mam doesn't realize how hard it is for a girl to get a place in a CA firm. It's always men, you know, who get the first crack at that sort of situation. And Mam hasn't studied the *Professional Vacancy* columns in the paper the way I have. She just doesn't realize that business isn't good enough these days for Accountancy to be much in demand. Besides, the CA exams aren't all *that* easy to pass."

"But you boasted to the Earl about how well you'd done the farm books. And you *are* good at that sort of thing."

"Well of course I did! I had to put on a bit of a show, hadn't I, to get this reference out of him? But that was still only a piddling little job that doesn't really prove anything. And how can you be sure I'd be good at the big Accountancy jobs when I'm not even sure of it myself?"

"I'm not. I can't be, of course. But you aren't even going to try. You said that. You said you're not even going to stay long enough at the Academy to take your Highers."

"That's right," Linda agreed. "And suppose I hadn't said that? He'd just have told me to come back in a year's time when I *had* sat them. Wouldn't he? But I mightn't have been able to see him another year, like I did today, because there's no certainty that you'll be working there another winter—which means you wouldn't be so pally with Ramenski that he'd arrange it for you. That's all there was to that part of it. And so why all the song and dance about my spinning a yarn to get what I wanted?"

It all hung together so well, it sounded so logical. And of course, Linda knew so much more than she did about it all, that she just couldn't think of any more arguments. But she still had to have the assurance that Linda wasn't really deceiving her, and so she asked,

"But you will tell Mam about it, won't you? You will explain to her about this hotel thing being just a standby in case you can't get into Accountancy?"

"Yes, yes." Linda was becoming impatient, making her feel she had been stupid over the whole business. "But for heaven's sake, Jinty, I can't get into arguments with her before I sit my term exams—especially with Meg due to sit her Highers at the same time. How

193

could either of us concentrate on exam study with Mam nagging away all the time about her precious ambitions for me? So just keep your mouth shut, will you, and let me choose my own time to tell her."

Everybody seemed to be ordering her to keep her mouth shut—her mother, Mr. Ramenski, and now Linda. And yet—It was easier that way. She didn't want to get into rows and arguments. All she wanted was to wear her green suit and enjoy it, and let the rest of them get on as well as they could with all their problems.

The first time she wore the suit was on Easter Sunday, walking to church with the rest of the family and feeling not only equal to Meg and Linda at last, but even— in the newness and grace of her appearance that day— just a little bit superior to them. The cream-colored straw hat Meg had loaned her was perfect with the suit, too; and with a sideways smile at the effect of it all, Meg told her,

"You look pretty, young 'un. Linda has good taste."

"And Jinty has backbone," their mother said. "She worked hard all winter to earn that suit."

Their father grinned at this interchange. "Aye, you're growing up," he told her. And then, a lot more soberly, he added, "You'll soon have all the troubles your sisters have."

That last remark meant he was thinking about the exam week in May, and the amount of time Meg and Linda were having to spend in studying for it. They were all aware of that; and in the words, too, they realized, there was a hint of his feelings about the atmosphere developing in their house because of that week. He didn't like it. He disapproved of the tension building up out of their mother's attitude towards it; and already there had been one occasion when they had overheard him saying irritably,

"Dammit, Jean, do you have to make such a sacred cow out of these exams?"

"They're important to the girls. You know they are."

"All right, then. But why d'you have to hover over them the way you do when they're studying? You can't sit the exams for them, can you? So why don't you let them alone to get on with it?"

Treading sedately to church that morning, very conscious of the way her high heels made her green skirt swirl with every step, she wished momentarily that her mother would give up worrying about the exams; and, at the same time, knew she might as well wish for the moon. Her mother was so terribly set on both Linda and Meg going on to take a University degree; and that couldn't happen for Meg until she'd cleared the hurdle of Highers. As for Linda, she wouldn't even be allowed to try for Highers next year unless she passed well enough in her term exams.

A dreadful thought struck her. Supposing that something should go terribly wrong for one of them in that important week, and all her mother's dreams for that one came toppling in ruins? *"I don't want to see you girls suffering my regrets. . . ."* The conversations she'd had with her mother in the woods began to echo in her mind. The picture she had built up of the solemn young girl in the confectionery shop began to haunt her; and in the growing fear of either Meg or Linda failing in their exams, she began to worry in proportion to her mother's worry.

"But we'll not fail," Meg assured her when she eventually voiced this fear on the night before the first of the exams. "We're both pretty sure of good passes in everything, in fact."

And yet, she thought, Meg didn't *look* confident. Meg had been unusually tense and nervous for weeks past. And she'd been having moods, too, which was also unusual for her—melancholy one day, and bursting with high spirits the next. Their mother also seemed to have noticed the moods, because there wasn't once in the week of the exams that she pestered either Meg or Linda to tell how they thought they'd done in that day's papers. It wasn't until the afternoon of the day it was all over, in fact, that she started to question them, and then took off in soaring high spirits herself when they both said they were sure they'd passed well in all the papers. But the high spirits didn't last, because it was on the evening of that day also, that Meg said,

"Mam, I wish you'd stop talking about my going on to University now."

"But why?" Their mother looked a little hurt at first, then puzzled; but finally she laughed and said, "Oh, I know I do go on, but it's just that I'm so pleased for you. I'm sorry, Meg. I know you must be terribly tired after all that effort."

"I'm tired, too; dead tired," Linda said. "And if I hear another word about Meg going on to be a teacher and myself going on to be a CA, I think I'll scream."

"Point taken," their mother said ruefully. "You'd better get to bed, the pair of you."

"Not yet," Meg said. She looked more nervous than ever now, and something in the tone of her voice made their father put down his newspaper to stare at her. Meg glanced from him to their mother, and said,

"Mam, Dad, I've something to tell you. I worked hard to pass my Highers because I knew that meant so much to Mam, and because she's sacrificed a lot to make that possible. But I'm not going on to University. I don't want to."

"What do you want, Meg?" Their father spoke first, holding up a hand to check the spate of exclamation that would otherwise have burst from their mother. Meg turned gratefully towards him. Quietly, her lips trembling a little on the words, she said,

"I want to be married, Dad. To Dave Ferguson."

"What?" Their mother was on her feet with the word, shocked anger in her face. "Have you been seeing that fellow again? After all I said to you about him!"

Meg rose to face her. "What do you think, Mam?" she asked. "I'm not made of wood. And you can't carve and shape me like a piece of wood, the way Dad carves his little toy animals. Of course I've been seeing him. I love him."

"Wait, now! Wait!" Again their father checked the rush of reply from their mother. "You've got to let the girl speak, Jean."

"Yes, Mam," Meg said. "You never would before, when I tried to tell you about Dave's plans. But you must now. He's always wanted a garage business of his own, and now he's got one—or one that's partly his, at least. It's in Haimston. He didn't have the capital to buy it, but Tom Meikle wanted to go into partnership with him. Archie Meikle agreed to that, because soon there won't be enough trade at the smithy for both him and Tom—not with all the mechanization of farm work that's been going on. And so, to make it possible for Tom to go in with Dave, Archie has put up the money to buy the business."

She paused, looking from the quivering outrage of their mother's expression to the listening intentness of their father's face. "And what I want now," she finished, "is to be married to Dave and help him to build up the business. And have our children—Dave's and mine. That's what we both want."

"But, Meg, your career—"

"But, Meg, you were just seventeen in February past—"

Their father and their mother spoke together, voices cutting across one another. Their father's voice won the battle; and he went on, "—and that's awful young to marry, girl. He's a good lad, Dave, I know; and he seems to have sensible ideas. But he's very young, too, and people's feelings change as they grow older. I doubt you'll have to wait a year or so yet, dearie, before we could let you have our permission to marry."

"She'll not have mine then, I can tell you!" The words waiting to burst from their mother would not be denied now. They came tumbling out, hard, fast, and furious. "You're a fool, Meg—a stupid, sentimental fool! And ungrateful as well. I've slaved my whole married life to let you have a good education, just so that you could have the chance that's yours for the taking now; the chance of a career, independence, the right to live well off your own earnings, to *do* something with your life. And you throw it right back at me with all this talk about drudging away your young years for the sake of some village lout who thinks he can run a garage. But you'll never get my permission for that, Meg. Never, never, never! I'd die first—like I nearly did when you were born. But I'll never let you waste your life like mine has—"

"*Mam!*" Meg was screaming to make herself heard, her face as distorted as their mother's. "*Mam, stop, please stop!*"

"Yes, stop it, Jean." Their father rose in one swift lunge that brought him to stand between the two of them, forcing them to back from one another. Meg looked up at him. Her voice came in a whisper now, instead of a scream.

"I knew it would be like this with Mam," the whisper said. "I just knew it would."

"Well, it doesn't have to be," their father told her. He was angry now, and anger was so rare with him that they were all momentarily silenced. "Your mother has always done as she thought fit for you, and I've always understood her reasons for that. What's more, it's because I understood that I've never interfered in her plans, or helped her with them either. But I'm going to interfere now, by God, because nobody will ever get the chance to say I'm not the man in my own house."

With a swift stride to where his jacket hung, he unhooked it and made for the door, talking over his shoulder to their mother as he went.

"I'm off to the smithy to ask Tom Meikle for a lift down to the Hall to see Dave Ferguson's father. We'll sort this out between us, I promise you."

"Dad, please!" Meg called out as he turned away to the door. "Wait, Dad. I want to tell you—"

"No!" their father interrupted. "For once, Meg, I'll tell you. I'm not dead set against your marrying, the way your mother is. But I still think it's better for you and Dave to wait a year or two. And I'm going to make sure you do. This very night, I'll make sure!"

"But, Dad," Meg cried. "You can't! You just can't do that now—"

It was no use. He was gone, and Meg was speaking to empty air. Their mother sat down beside the table, her hands blindly picking at threads in the table cover. "I don't know what to say." The hands went on picking at the cloth as she repeated, "I don't know what to say." She looked old; defeated. Meg hovered around with a sort of baffled despair on her face. Then, like someone coming suddenly to a decision, she sat down at the opposite side of the table and said,

"Mam, listen to me, please. There's a lot more I

haven't said yet, and it can't wait till Dad comes back."

"It'll have to wait." Sharply their mother drew back from the hand Meg was reaching out towards her own restless fingers. "You heard him. He'll be man in his own house. And he's entitled to that, isn't he?"

"But, Mam—" Meg began again, and then checked herself, with a shrug and a sigh of frustration. Their mother looked down again at the table cover. Meg leaned her head on her hand and sat staring into space. From the corner where she had sat since the row began, Linda watched them both, her eyes going from one to the other. A minute passed in silence; two minutes, five. As the silence in the room grew deeper, Linda's face took on a grim, calculating look. Another minute passed; and then Linda spoke.

15

"Mam," Linda said, "revelations seem to be in the air, and so you'd better have mine, too. I'm not going on to sit my Highers next year, and that means I won't be going to University either."

Their mother's head came up slowly till her eyes met those of Linda. In a voice of slow, dull wonder, she asked, "You've not— You're not tied up, too, with some silly boy—are you?"

"Don't be daft!" Linda's tone was contemptuous. "I've just looked hard at the options I have, that's all. And the way the market is now, I don't stand a chance of getting into a CA firm."

Their mother began the old, familiar argument. "But you're good at that sort of thing—"

"So are a lot of people." Brutally Linda cut across the first words of it. "And with the competition I'd have to face, not even a degree could get me into Accountancy."

"But you've got brains—you'd take a good degree,"

their mother began again; and again, Linda pressed on,

"Yes, yes. But that's not the point, Mam. I know very well how much you want all of us to have professional careers; but slaving for years to get a degree, and then begging for a chance to enter a CA firm isn't my idea of the good life. There's a much better, quicker way for me to reach all the things you want for us. I'm going into hotel work. I asked the Earl for a reference—"

"You did *what*?"

"I asked him for a reference to Forsyth International Hotels. He's Chairman of the Board—you must know that. He gave me a good one; and I've used it, Mam. There's a job open for me in one of their London hotels as soon as I let the manager know I've passed this year's exams. And now that I'm sure I have, I'm going to take that job."

"But you don't need your standard of education for a clerking job in a hotel," their mother protested. "And that's the only kind you'd get at your age. It would be wasting your talents, Linda; just wasting them."

Linda shook her head, her lips set in a tight little smile of triumph. "No," she said. "No, Mam; not at all. Clerking will be only a part of it, for me. I've been taken on as a trainee manager. I'll learn every department of the hotel—not just the clerking. I'll travel; go to Forsyth hotels all over the world. And I'll finish up as the boss! I can't fail to do that. I won't fail. D'you understand, Mam? I'll get to the top—*my* way; but I'll still get there. And that was what you wanted, wasn't it?"

Their mother looked at Linda in silence for a moment before she said, "Yes, Linda, I believe you will get to the top. You're determined enough for that. But why didn't you tell me about all this? I can see the reasoning that's decided you to destroy my dream for you. But why this way? Why did you have to creep behind my back to do it?"

Sudden rage flooded Linda's face. "Because you wouldn't have listened!" she shouted. "Because it's the same with me as it is with Meg. You've always been so obsessed with making both of us over into some image of what *you* might have been, that you *can't* listen. That's why!"

Their mother's back stiffened, as if some of her old fighting spirit had suddenly revived. "I'd have listened," she said coldly, "long enough at least to let you know the kind of life you'd have to lead in a hotel; the long hours you'd have to work—not to mention the fact that a girl of your age in that setting is the natural prey of any man who takes his fancy where it pleases—"

"I can work," Linda interrupted. "I've never been afraid of work. And you won't get me throwing my cap over the windmill for any man. I'm not as daft as Meg, you know."

Meg . . . Their mother's eyes flashed to the clock on the wall. "That's enough, Linda," she commanded. "Your father's due back any second now; and I can't deal with you before I'm sure he's got this business of Meg sorted out."

Linda opened her mouth to protest again, but before she could utter more than a word, Meg said,

"Mam, Dad can't sort it out. Nobody can. That's something you're just going to have to accept."

Their mother shook her head. "You're wrong there," she retorted. "You'll not see that fellow Ferguson again, Meg. Not while I live, at least."

"I will see Dave," Meg told her quietly. "I'll see him for the rest of my life, Mam, because—" She paused, swallowed hard, and then finished, "—because of what I wanted to tell you and Dad when neither of you would listen to me. I'm expecting Dave's baby."

Their mother jerked backward in her chair, mouth open, breath coming hard through it. Her lips worked, trying to shape words. "You—you—" Meg flushed scarlet; but it was Linda who broke into the stuttered words; Linda with her own resentment openly showing in the spiteful voice that goaded,

"Go on, then. Tell her what that makes her. Because you know, don't you? You know all about having a bastard."

Their mother froze where she sat, her face, her whole body, rigid in shock. Then slowly her head moved, turning from Meg to Linda, and back to Meg again. She looked dazed, still, as she said to Meg,

"You told her. You told Linda."

"But I didn't, I didn't!" Meg was weeping now. Chokingly, through her sobs, she went on protesting, "How could I, when I didn't really know it myself till now? You didn't tell me outright when you spoke to me that night after I sneaked out to the kirn. You just gave me hints, warnings, about the way things could happen.

205

And it wasn't till I put the hints together with other things that I guessed about it. But I still never said a word to *her!*"

Their mother turned to Linda. "Then how did you know?"

"I needed my birth certificate," Linda said defiantly, "to send away with my application for the hotel job. I went raking for it in the box where you keep all those papers. I found Meg's birth certificate, too."

"Oh, God!" Their mother gasped the words, holding her hands up before her head as if she were warding off blows. And Linda didn't show any mercy. Linda went on hammering blows at her.

"So you're quite clever yourself, aren't you, when it comes to deceiving people? *Father unknown*—that's what it says on Meg's birth certificate—*Father unknown.*"

"It wasn't—" Their mother began to speak, lowering her arms to show the white, distraught face they had hidden. "It wasn't like that. He was—I—" She gasped, unable to say any more of the words choking in her throat.

Oh, why couldn't she speak? Why couldn't she manage to tell about the young soldier being killed before she could marry him?

"You bitch, Linda! You cruel bitch!" Meg was on her feet, shouting at Linda. Linda shouted back at her, and all the time under the sound of their quarrelling there was that gasping noise of their mother's effort to form words.

"*Roger Belaney, Roger Belaney.*" She mouthed the name, silently willing her mother to look at her doing so; willing her to explain to Linda about the War, to tell Linda that everything about Meg hadn't been squalid the way it sounded with that *Father unknown* label on it. Meg's father wasn't unknown. He was Roger Belaney, and her mother had truly been in love with him.

Her mother didn't see her. None of them was paying any attention to her, crouching down by the fireplace and shaking like a leaf from it all. She couldn't stand any more of it. She started to uncurl herself so that she could bolt upstairs, and the movement brought her around to look straight at Archie Meikle standing in the doorway of the room. Her mother had also realized his presence. Her mother was rising to her feet and asking shakily,

"How did you get in here?"

"Your man left the front door wide open behind him. I thought I was expected to come straight in. And I did."

"And how long have you been standing there?"

Archie nodded towards Linda and Meg. "Since just before these two started the row over what Linda had said to you."

So Archie Meikle knew about the birth certificate! She could see her mother stiffening at the realization; the strength visibly flowing back to her with the need to keep the Morrison family's business from the ears of gossip-mongers. Her mother spoke again, in a voice that was harsh now, and strong.

"Then I'm warning you, Archie Meikle. You'd better not speak of what you heard. And why is your Tom not back with my husband?"

"He will be, any minute now, mistress. And as for what I heard, I'm hardly likely to gossip about it now, after I've kept my mouth close-shut on it these seventeen years past."

Her mother gasped. "You're lying!" she exclaimed. "Nobody knew except for myself and two others. And you were never one of those!"

"Look, Mistress Morrison." Archie was beginning to sound annoyed. "I didn't come to talk about this, but I won't be called a liar. You've forgotten that I'm a lot older than you, and that I've known the Earl all my life—"

"*He* told you?"

"No, no. Ballinford's the last man to betray a confidence. But young Belaney was his own cousin's son— remember? And there was many a time I saw him on his visits to the Hall when he was just a wee laddie and I was a young man going back and forth to do farrier work in the stables there. We got quite friendly, in fact. He even wrote to me during the War to tell me about getting engaged to the girl who had nursed him in some hospital in England, and to invite me to the wedding that never happened. And then, when you came here with your two eldest after the Earl had given your husband his job, I knew Meg for Belaney's child the minute I clapped eyes on her."

Her mother stared at Archie, silently, anguish twisting her face. They were all staring—herself, Meg, Linda. There was a sort of wonder written on Meg's face. Linda's eyes were narrowed in curiosity.

"It wasn't hard to guess the reason for the job, either," Archie added. "The Earl was fond of Roger Belaney, but he never spoke to that branch of the family again, after the lad was killed. That made me pretty sure they had turned their backs on you, and that a job for your husband was his way of helping you out."

Still her mother didn't speak to him. She turned to Linda instead, and said wearily, "Well, you've heard it all now—except for two things. He was ordered back to his regiment just thirty-six hours before our wedding; and the very next day after that, he was killed."

"I'm sorry," Linda said.

Their mother nodded. "It would be strange if you weren't." They stood looking at one another. "Go to bed now, Linda," the weary voice went on at last. "And Linda, your father will miss you when you go off to that hotel job, but he won't mind your taking it. Start packing for it tomorrow."

Linda looked taken aback for a moment, then she recovered herself and said defiantly, "You can't throw me out like that. I'll go when I'm ready."

"You'll go as soon as your father knows about the job," their mother told her, "because it's him I'm thinking about now, Linda. He loved me enough to give Meg his name. And d'you think that you and he and I could live under the same roof with the knowledge of what you've made out of that?"

"But I was angry at the time," Linda protested. "I couldn't help myself. And anyway, you needn't tell him."

"No, not if you go quickly. But do you really think I could hide it from him if you don't?"

Linda had no answer then, except for a shrug. For a moment or two after that, she stood there, hovering between uncertainty and defiance. Defiance won. She shrugged again, and said,

"Well, why not? I'm onto a sure thing, after all." She walked to the door, her step brisk and confident, and at the door she turned and said, "D'you remember I told you once how quickly I'd take advantage of a sure thing?"

It was to Meg she spoke. But it wasn't a question that needed an answer; and Meg didn't give one. Instead, she moved to their mother, and said,

"Mam, I'm sorry it had to happen like this—me and Linda, both on the same night. But it's not the way you think it is with me, Mam. I'm—"

"Wait!" Brusquely cutting across Meg's words, their mother turned to Archie Meikle. "I take it you came here to speak about that money you've loaned to your Tom," she said. "Is that so?"

"Aye; but there's more to it than that," Archie told her. "And since Meg doesn't seem to have got the chance to tell you the rest, I'd better do it for her. Your Meg was a married woman before she started that baby, Mistress Morrison. I married her and Dave across my anvil."

Their mother looked blank at first, as if she hadn't been able to take this in. Then, with her features working in the first of realization, she exclaimed,

"*You* married her! So it was your fault. You were the start of it all. My God, Archie Meikle, d'you know what you're saying? What *do* you have to say for yourself now?"

Archie scratched his head. "Nothing much," he admitted. "She and Dave wanted to marry. I saw nothing against it. Neither did Tom and his wife, or they wouldn't have acted as witnesses for the two of them."

"You knew *I* was against it. You all knew that. And if you didn't already know, Meg must have told you. Why else would she have come to you?"

"Oh, she told me that, all right," Archie agreed. "Said she might be able to persuade her Dad; but you— never. And you'd have heard about it, if the banns had been published as they would have had to be for a church wedding, or for one in the Registry Office. And so there was nothing for it except an anvil wedding."

"And you went ahead with that, instead of coming to tell me that she'd asked you for it! Have you no conscience, Archie Meikle?"

"Now look, Mistress Morrison," Archie exclaimed. "Sixteen is the legal age for marriage without consent of parents—or it is in this country, at least. And you don't seem to realize the determination that's in this girl of yours. If I hadn't married her when she and Dave asked me to do that, she'd just have run away from home so that she could get someone else to marry them. And then she'd have missed the exams you set such store on, wouldn't she? Besides—"

His rapid flow of words faltered. He turned to look at Meg. Meg nodded to him, and said,

"I'll say it, Mr. Meikle."

"Say what?" Their mother's glance went from one to the other. Meg held the glance with her own, and said,

"I've tried every way I know to get you to agree to me marrying Dave; and tonight, you still refused me. I knew it would be like that; and so I told Archie that, whether he married us or not, I meant to start a baby. That's when he gave in and married us."

"You see?" Archie asked. "That meant there was the unborn to think of, as well. And who am I to deny any bairn its daddy?"

"And who are you to make decisions for me!"

Their mother whipped round on Archie with the words, face flushed, eyes brilliant with anger. "You!" she stormed. "You took my daughter from me. It still wasn't too late to do something about her and that boy when she came to you. It still wasn't too late to save her for the kind of life *I* meant her to have. I'll never forgive you this, Archie Meikle. Never, never . . ."

The storming voice went on and on, filling the room, making the air in it seem like a thick fog of pain, and anger, and despair. And then, from nowhere, it seemed, the room was suddenly full of people—Dave Ferguson's father, her own father, Tom Meikle, and Dave himself. They were all talking, all arguing, all trying to make themselves heard, one above the other. Fragments of the argument hurtled at her out of the din—"but don't you understand, yet? She's *pregnant* by him!" That was her mother, shrieking the words into her father's face. Tom Meikle, shouting as much as anyone, kept telling them to be calm; it could all be talked over calmly. Archie was at her father's shoulder saying over and over again, "But she *is* married—truly married." And John Ferguson was roaring that Dave was a good boy, Dave's folks would stand by him; while her father, groaning and holding his hands over his ears kept protesting, "Let me think, let me *think!*"

Then, as suddenly as it seemed to have started, it was all over. Meg and Dave, the only two who had not taken part in the row, were standing together in the center of the room, facing all the others. Dave had his arms around Meg, and he was saying quietly,

"We didn't intend you to learn about it like this. We had it planned that I should be the one to tell you, but Meg couldn't help herself speaking out tonight. And now we're going."

"That's right, Morrison," John Ferguson said angrily. "If your wife can't treat the girl properly, Dave's mother will. And so will I!"

"But, Meg—" It was terrible to see how bewildered their father looked, stretching his hand first to Meg and then to their mother. "I don't want you to go, Meg. I don't want to lose you."

Meg clutched at the hand hovering between herself and their mother. "I don't want to go, Dad," she said shakily. "Not this way. Not till Dave and I can be married again, in church. And I won't go till then, if Mam wants it that way too."

Everybody looked at their mother. Her face was like a mask; white, grim, unyielding. The stiff lips in the mask moved, formed words.

"Meg's made her own bed. Let her lie on it. She's no daughter of mine now."

A shuffling sound as everyone trooped awkwardly out, a glimpse of violet-blue eyes as Meg turned her head to give a final, forlorn look of appeal; then it was over. There were only the three of them left in the room; her father striking his fist in his hand with despair, her mother standing stockstill with that unyielding look on her face, and herself crouching forgotten in her corner by the fire.

Quietly she slipped from the room, and went up the attic stairs. In the attic itself she found suitcases strewn about, and Linda lying in Meg's bed. Linda had listened in to the row, and she knew Meg wouldn't be coming back. The double bed was cold and comfortless, and she felt very much alone.

16

Everything about the house was lonely now, and the fresh paint, the new curtains—all the things that had been so dear to her mother's heart, only seemed to make it more so.

Linda wrote from London, scribbling her letters on hotel notepaper. They were casual letters, brief, and spiked with acidly comic remarks about people she'd met in the hotel, people she worked with there. They all read Linda's letters, and even her mother laughed sometimes at the comedy in them. But it was her father who really enjoyed them. Linda would go far, he said, and it had been a wise decision to let her take the job. But her father, of course, still didn't know how that decision had been forced; and every time he spoke about Linda, the closed expression on her mother's face was like a sign saying that he never would know.

Meg wrote, too, from Haimston where she and Dave had rented a house after the church wedding that

Dave's folks had arranged for them. But whether Meg's letters were read or not was something that no one could tell, because her mother always put them away unopened; and after a while, Meg stopped writing. Then, one day, there was a letter from Meg for herself, and her mother didn't stop her reading that. But she couldn't write back, because Meg didn't give her address in Haimston.

"Not that I don't want to," the letter said, *"but just in case you decide to visit me—which would mean that you'd be in Mam's bad books if you told her about it, or maybe mixed up in a lot of lies if you didn't."*

She took the problem to Archie Meikle, and Archie said, "Well, you're at school in Haimston, aren't you? And so what's to stop you seeing Meg there 'by accident,' as it were? If she came walking by the school gates, perhaps, or the bus stop. Just at the time you happened to be there—eh?"

It wasn't much of an arrangement, just meeting like that for a few minutes at a time. And of course, it needed Tom Meikle and Dave to act the part of go-between, so that she knew when she could expect to see Meg coming towards her. All the same, it was still the only one that would allow her to keep out of trouble at home; and it was enough, at least, to tell her that having a baby suited Meg. The more her figure plumped out, in fact, the more beautiful she became; and speaking of home was the only thing that seemed to be able to dim her radiance. But not entirely, of course. The bouncy cheerfulness so natural to Meg wouldn't allow of that.

"Just you wait, Jinty," she kept saying. "Wait till Mam actually sees the baby. She won't be able to resist then!"

But what hope could there be of that happening when her mother would never take the first step towards it, and the doors of their house were closed against Meg? In the deserted silence of the attic room that seemed so big and bare to her now, she tried to figure out all the possibilities; and it was there, also, that she worked secretly on the jacket she was knitting as a present for Meg's baby.

"You don't go out enough, Jinty," her mother scolded. "All that time by yourself in the attic. It's not good for you."

"I don't want to go out more," she said. "And in any case, I couldn't go anywhere special now, could I?"

Nowhere special—not even to the end of term school dance, where she had meant to cut such a fine figure in her green suit, instead of having to wear her old party dress. The suit was a thing of the past now. She'd burned it, one night when she was alone in the house, using the big kitchen scissors to cut it into inch-square pieces and then scattering these like green confetti on the fire. The new shoes had followed, then the new handbag—all her winter's work melting into black, crumbling into ashes.

And how her heart had ached to see it happen! But

she still had to punish herself for being stupid enough to let Linda deceive her into arranging the interview with the Earl. She still had to get rid of the guilt she felt over the way that she had contributed to the terrible night of the family row. And she had no way of making amends except through that ache.

"I'll never understand," her mother sighed. "You worked so hard for that suit, Jinty, and it was so pretty. I'll never understand why you took such a sudden dislike to it."

She shrugged, keeping up the pretense that it had been only a stupid whim, trying to pass it off by saying she would earn more money next winter.

"Aye, if there's any to be had," her mother said darkly, because the Hall was closed up now. Lord Garvald was away at some college in England working at a year's course on Estate Management—the first time he had ever been allowed to study away from home, instead of having tutors come to him; and the Earl had gone to live near the college, to make sure Garvald didn't do anything dangerous enough to get himself killed. That was what they said in the village, anyway; but Archie Meikle didn't believe the Hall would be shut up for the whole year of Lord Garvald's course.

"There'll be Christmas holidays at that college, won't there?" he demanded. "What's more, Lord Garvald has his twenty-first birthday in January. The Earl's bound to have a party for that, and where else would a

Ballinford have his coming-of-age party but at the Hall?"

"Archie's kidding himself," her father said. "It would cost a mint to open the Hall just for a few weeks in the winter."

But wasn't the Earl noted for his extravagant gestures? When harvest time went past, with only Mr. Nelson there to wave corn dolly aloft, she felt a sense of loss that made her wish Archie would be proved right after all; but even so, it still wasn't that possibility which came first in her mind. Meg's baby was due at the end of December, and when she was walking home from the smithy one day with her father he had told her quietly that he would take her up to the hospital at Haimston to see Meg and the baby. Provided she didn't let dab about it to her mother, he added. As if she would be so stupid!

It was frosty that day, the sharpest frost she had ever known. Then the snow came, and as she ticked off the December days on her attic calendar the weather settled in for the hardest, whitest winter that anyone could remember. There was a snowplow clearing the road ahead of them when they eventually caught the bus to visit the hospital; but inside the hospital itself was warm and bright, and the brightest thing of all there was the red-gold of Meg's hair spread out against the great pile of white pillows supporting her as she sat up with the baby in her arms.

It was a girl, a little scrap of a thing, with a thatch

of downy gold and a face so comically like a crumpled version of Dave's face grinning down at it, that she and her father both had to laugh at the sight. Everybody exclaimed over the knitted jacket that was her present for it. Then Meg let her hold the baby, smiling at the cautious way she took it in her arms. And Meg smiling like that, Meg looking up so ripe and warm and tender from her nest of pillows, was more beautiful than she had ever been.

"You're an aunt now, Jinty," she said, and this raised another laugh—from all of them, this time. But it wasn't all so cheerful, of course; not when Meg asked,

"Dad, does Mam know you're here?"

"She's guessed at it, I think," he answered. "I didn't say anything, but she must have guessed when we took the Haimston bus in this weather."

"She'll come round." Meg laid a reassuring hand on his arm. "She's got to, Dad, for her own sake."

Dave was playing with the baby, enchanted by the grip it had achieved on his forefinger, but he looked up long enough to agree, "Aye, Mr. Morrison. Just wait it out like we're doing, and you'll be a proper granda yet."

They went away from the ward with her father saying, "He's a good lad, that Dave. And did you ever see Meg look so bonny?"

"Never, Dad," she said; and was glad that her mother had insisted on Linda going straight off to the hotel job. It was bad enough, she thought, for her father to be missing both Meg and Linda so much without him

also having to know of the cruel way Linda had be-
haved before she left.

They got off the bus at the smithy to find Archie
holding forth to all the men comfortably established by
the warmth of the forge, and a great air of pleased
excitement in the place.

"Aye, John Morrison! And what did I tell you?"
Archie broke off what he was saying to shout triumphantly as they appeared in the doorway of the
smithy. "The Earl's back, my mannie! He's opened the
Hall for young Garvald's twenty-first, and you're invited to the party. We're all invited. The whole dam'
village is going to it!"

They got the details of Archie's news, bit by bit, as
all the other men added their contributions. The Earl
was really going to do things in style, it seemed. He
had brought hired staff up from the south with him, to
cope with the party. He had engaged an orchestra to
play at it, and the invitation was open to every single
person on his estates. And because the ice on the lake
in the Hall gardens was bearing, that was where the
party was to be held—on the ice, with skating, and
curling, and dancing to the orchestra, fairy lights strung
from the trees around the lake, a buffet, and champagne for everyone. It was to be the biggest, the most
extravagant yet of all his extravagant gestures.

"And very likely," Archie said gleefully, "the only
living soul who *won't* be there to enjoy it is our dear
minister. Because you wouldn't get old Hell-fire at an
occasion like that—now, would you?"

Nobody cared to contradict Archie on that, after he had been proved so right about everything else. But Archie had forgotten that Mr. Elphinston approved of Lord Garvald as much as he disapproved of the Earl; and Mr. Elphinston was there, even though he drank only tea instead of the champagne that was offered to him. Furthermore, Mr. Elphinston turned out to have been a champion curler in his youth, and most of his time at the party was spent on the curling rink marked out at one side of the lake.

The Hall was all lit up, just like it had been in the winter she had worked there; but instead of a darkness of trees fringing the gravelled drive around the lake, there was an airy pattern of branches showing like black lace against the sparkle of fairy lights, and the lights themselves were like a brilliant, multi-colored reflection of the silver star pattern high above the trees. The buffet had been set up at the side of the lake nearest to the Hall. The orchestra faced the buffet across the breadth of the lake. The ice between was thronged with moving figures, people skating, throwing curling stones, a long line of children sliding. She ran ahead of her father and mother when the sound of it all began to reach them, and stopped at the end of the familiar path through the trees as the whole scene opened out like some bright patchwork before her. The orchestra was playing a waltz—"The Blue Danube." Her mother came up behind her, exclaiming,

"D'you hear it! Oh, when I think how I used to dance to that!"

Her father said, "I wonder if there's any beer at that buffet."

Beer, when there was champagne for the asking! As she broke away from the two of them to run towards the ice, she laughed to hear her mother scolding him in those very words. Then she was at the lakeside, cautiously testing the shining, whitish-gray surface of the ice before she began running across it; and over the talking, laughing voices all around as she sailed down the long, gleaming line of the slide, "The Blue Danube" was a shrill sweet loudness of violins rhythmically rising and falling in time to her own run and glide and swoop and glide and run. . . .

The musicians were wearing red jackets. The wind-players' instruments were a solid gleam of gold against the red. And all of them, too, were drinking champagne. She could see waiters standing with trays of glasses all ready to hand out to them when they came to the end of their waltz. To the left of the slide, where the curlers were, Mr. Elphinston was showing ferocious skill in his aim with a curling stone; and from the other end of the rink, when the stone landed there, Archie Meikle began yelling for a second stone to be placed where it would protect the position of the first one.

"A guard! A guard!" Hoarse and frantic, Archie's voice came echoing down the ice. "We need a guard, minister!"

We need a guard! Archie must be dead keen on curling to team up like that with old Hell-fire! A line of young men and women skaters appeared, each one in the line holding to the waist of the person in front. Lord Garvald was their leader, and the line snaked and wavered behind him till it broke up in confusion and laughter, with all the young men and women pairing off eventually to join in the waltzing. Twice, the Earl glided by, the first time with a pretty young woman on his arm, the second time with his hands linked in those of his sister, Lady Staneford. He was wearing his usual old tweeds. Between exertion and the coldness of the air, his face was ruddier than ever; and bearing down with the trim and slender Lady Staneford linked to him like this, he looked like a battered pirate-hulk with an elegant prize ship in tow. He was talking, and she caught his words as he went by.

"Yes, madam. The wages of sin is death."

Why? she wondered. Why, in the midst of all this enjoyment and laughter, had he harked back to the words Mr. Elphinston had once thrown at him?

A space suddenly cleared on the ice as a girl and a young man, both dressed in skintight black and silver, came dashing from the edge of the lake. There was a loud chord from the orchestra before they broke into another series of waltzes. The black and silver figures glided, jumped, pirouetted, with all the graceful lordliness of professionals among amateurs; and by the time their display was over, she was dying to have a shot at skating, herself. But where was she to get hold of a pair of skates? She went to the buffet instead, and saw that Mr. Ramenski was in charge there. His dark, melancholy face lit up in a smile when he saw her; and with one hand reaching out to a tray of filled glasses, he asked,

"You like some champagne, Jinty—yes?"

She eyed the glass longingly. It was fragile, slender-stemmed, and there were little bubbles breaking up through the gold of the champagne in its shallow cup. But she had never tasted wine before, and she was a little afraid of what it might do to her.

"I might get drunk," she told Mr. Ramenski; and gravely, he said,

"If you do, I have you arrested. Or put in hospital, maybe."

He was joking, of course; but there were two police-men standing not far from him, and before she came up to the buffet she had noticed two men from the St. John's Ambulance Brigade patrolling the edge of the lake. She took the wine, laughing at Mr. Ramenski's joke about it, but still thinking that the Earl had left nothing at all to chance in making the party a success—not even the possibility of an accident on the ice, or someone getting fighting drunk on unlimited champagne. Mr. Ramenski plied her with the food kept hot under the great silver covers she could remember polishing so often before then. She ate ravenously, but only sipped at the champagne, wary of its unaccustomed taste and of the bubbles that fizzed up her nose.

"You are enjoying yourself?" Mr. Ramenski asked; and when she nodded and smiled, he said in a pleased way, "Tonight, all are enjoying themselves."

He was looking across the ice towards the Earl, she

noticed; and on impulse, she asked,

"What about him—the Earl? Is he all right now? I mean—" She hesitated, casting around for something that would sound more polite than the bald question, *"Is he still drinking?"* Mr. Ramenski looked puzzled for a moment, then he realized what was in her mind. With a quick look around to make sure no one else would hear him, he told her,

"No, no, Jinty. All that is past—except for tonight, maybe. Tonight he might get drunk on champagne—just to celebrate Lord Garvald's birthday, you understand. But not the other way. Not like it used to be, alone, and very sad."

"That's good," she said; and they smiled at one another, like old friends.

Her father came skating towards the buffet, holding up a pair of boots with skates attached to them. "Come on, Jinty!" he called. "I've borrowed boots and skates for both of us, and you're going to learn to use these."

He helped her on with the boots, then held her arm firmly and said, "Now all you do at first, is just walk—but without lifting your feet. Just like you were shuffling along with tiny steps—right?"

She tried that. Then, with the confidence born of his firm grip on her, she learned to lean into each step for the push that sent her gliding on the opposite foot—to lean, push, and glide again, left foot gliding, right foot gliding; slowly at first, then picking up pace until they were skimming rhythmically in step over the ice, with her father's arm guiding her when they twisted and turned among the other skaters. Faster and faster yet. So long as she remembered that left right, left right motion, so long as she was within the strong compass of his arm, there was no faltering in the long straight glides, no fear of the sweeping, circling turns.

"What waltz are they playing now?" she shouted; and her father shouted back,

"Waldteufel's 'Gold and Silver Waltz.' "

"Gold and silver, gold and silver . . ." She started to sing in time to the music. The fairy lights were like a spinning rainbow high over her head. The music was surging in waves of gold and silver, and she was riding the waves in a motion that felt like a mixture of flying and dancing. She laughed out loud with the sheer pleasure of it, and pushed impatiently at her father's hand, wanting suddenly to fly and dance by herself on the waves. But that was when her father began guiding her back to the edge of the lake, and saying as they went,

"That's enough, that's enough now. You're over-excited, my girl."

"I'm not, I'm not," she protested; but he was firm on that point. And besides, he pointed out, she'd had a long enough loan of the skates and it was high time to return them. Her shoes lay where she had left them; and when he had gone off with the borrowed skates in his hand, she sat lacing the shoes on and wondering what she might do next. Go in search of her mother, perhaps? She hadn't seen her mother once since they'd arrived at the party. She looked along the lakeside, and saw the Earl and Archie Meikle sitting side by side on the bank, talking to one another. They were enjoying themselves, she noticed, laughing and slapping one another on the back, and she thought they were probably having another one of their long conversations about the way things used to be when they were both young.

It had begun to snow again; soft, thick flakes of snow that piled up over everything like frosting. She stood up, brushing the snow from her shoulders. Her legs were trembling from the exertion of skating, she found, but once she had walked a few yards they were steady again. She went on, right around the lake, without catching sight of her mother. But that didn't matter now, she realized, because now she knew what she really wanted to do.

17

It had happened to her before, this feeling of all at once wanting to get away from noise and excitement, and just be by herself instead. "Sulking," her mother called it, but it wasn't true to say that. It was just an urge that came on her, as if she had suddenly reached a limit of what her mind could hold, and had to find a silent, lonely place where she could sit doing nothing, thinking of nothing.

The woods drew her, the darkness of the woods beyond the fairy lights; and even farther beyond that glitter, the vaster dark where the craggy outcrop they called Temple Rock rose steeply above the trees. The crag was easy to climb, except on its steep side, and often before then she had followed the small, crooked path leading to the ruins of the castle and the chapel on its summit. But there would be no need to go as far as that tonight. There was a tumble of boulders at the foot of the crag's steep side—huge boulders that leaned

229

against one another with cavelike spaces in between; and she could be very private there.

She walked on, with her eyes fixed on the looming shape of the crag. Then the trees closed round her, shutting off the sight of it, muffling the noise from the party till even the music was only a murmur, high-pitched and thin, like the ghost of music. The snow was absorbed by the great rim of dark around her, the spill of light from the lakeside was blotted out by it.

Walking through this part of the woods, she realized, was very different from following the path she and her mother had so often taken to the Hall. The trees all around her now were an ancient growth of beeches, tall, and huge in girth. There was no scrub here, no thin young trees that would have allowed for a filtering through of some of the light behind her, no paths to follow; nothing but these thick old trees rising from a carpet of snow-covered dead leaves that made her foot-steps almost soundless. She moved slowly, absorbing the quiet. This was the lonely place she had wanted. There was no point in going beyond it.

She stopped walking and sat down at the foot of one of the trees. Moss cushioned her. The wide spread of branches above protected her from the snow. The arch of tree root on either side of her rose high, like the sides of a heavy old armchair. She was tired now. She huddled back against the base of the tree, yielding thankfully to the tiredness, and gradually felt a great sense of sadness beginning to creep over her. But this was the part she liked about being alone, this sadness.

It was gentle, so gentle. It asked nothing from her. She huddled closer down between the tree roots, letting the sadness wash completely into her mind.

It was cold, sitting there. Very cold, she realized eventually; but the sadness was still there, holding her like a spell and making the cold seem a remote thing that didn't matter. Her mind began drifting towards some empty place of sleep. A sound broke into the emptiness, the faint sound of footsteps swishing through snow and dead leaves. Her mind was still working too slowly to feel fear. She looked towards the sound and saw a figure walking towards her—a man, a tall man. She stayed still. The man drew level, and stopped, staring down at her.

"Who the devil—!" It was the Earl. She'd have known his voice, even if she hadn't dimly recognized him by then. He stooped, peering more closely at her. "Good lord—it's you, Jinty! What the devil are you doing here?"

"Just being on my own." The truth sounded so stupid that she could only mutter it.

"But aren't you cold?" He didn't give her a chance to answer, but kept going on about how cold it was, how she ought to be getting back to her parents; and when she saw how he had to steady himself with one hand against the tree as he spoke, she realized that Lord Garvald's birthday meant he had got drunk after all. She felt inclined to laugh then, as she had laughed before at the talkative inclinations of other drunk men; but she was also pleased for him because his drinking that night hadn't been solitary, like those occasions in the library, and so she resisted this inclination.

"It was a good party," she offered. "I skated tonight, for the first time."

"Did you, b'God! And what was it like?"

"Great. A sort of cross between flying and dancing."

He laughed at that, and said, "Yes, I gave Garvald a bloody good send-off for his majority."

"A bloody good send-off," she agreed; but immediately he reproved her,

"Don't swear. You mustn't swear."

"You swear all the time," she pointed out; and he retorted,

"That's different. It's not nice to hear girls swearing."

She let that pass, and he went on talking in the same rambling way about Lord Garvald being on his own now that he was twenty-one, no longer being his or anyone else's responsibility.

"Legally of age, d'you see," he said. "The boy's legally of age now. Can't make him do a damn thing he doesn't want to do. Not any longer. No control over him. Can't look after him any more. All in the lap of the gods now."

She began to wish he would go away. It was making her uneasy to realize it was the thought of the Ballinford doom that lay behind every remark about Lord Garvald. The uneasiness transformed itself suddenly into the fey feeling that had come on her in the churchyard and in the library of the Hall; and she became so preoccupied with this that she no longer heard what the Earl was saying. It was only when he moved to sit astride the tree root arching on her right-hand side, that she became properly aware of him again. And he was still rambling on; about the village, this time, she gathered. She listened, putting in a remark of her own every now and then, and his monologue gradually became a conversation between them.

It was an unusual sort of conversation, too, she realized. What with the drink that had loosened his tongue, he seemed to be voicing his thoughts just as they came; and as for herself, she was too dazed with the cold to bother about her usual reserve with him. They were both talking on the same level, in fact; an unreal one that existed somewhere beyond the fact of their differing ages and social class. She let her mind drift at this level, forgetting she had wished he would go on to wherever he had been going; not minding, even, that long silences were also part of the strangeness of their conversation.

"Young Belaney was a fine lad," he said suddenly out of one of the silences. "I wish the truth about Meg hadn't come out the way it did."

"How d'you know about that?"

"Your mother. She came to see me to find out how Linda had got the reference out of me. She told me the whole story."

"Was she still just as upset then?"

"What d'you think? Meg was her love-child, her favorite. The moon and the stars together couldn't be good enough for Meg."

233

"And Linda? You could have smashed Linda's chances then, couldn't you?"

"Not for good. She's too determined for that. And not without having to admit myself a fool, in the process."

"It was hard on Mam—not just about Linda, but Meg too. And both on the same night."

"She's had it hard all her life, poor woman."

They talked again of Meg and Linda, later on, when some impulse of memory made her ask, "Why did you speak to Meg like that, the day we met you riding in the woods?"

"Speak like what?"

"About courage. You looked at her and said, *'That's what I should have expected, of course. Courage—the same kind.'*"

"Because I could see Roger Belaney so clearly in her, of course. And he was a young man who always had the courage to make his own life. Which is just what Meg's done, isn't it?"

"Linda made her own life, too."

"That's right. But it didn't take courage to do what she did—just ruthlessness. There's a big difference."

"I don't see it."

"Then it's time you did. The ruthless ones—it's just because they don't know what pity is that they can't know what fear is either. But there wouldn't be courage, would there, without fear? Because that's what courage is—a conquering of fear."

She tried to think clearly about all this, but her mind kept going off at a tangent that led her first towards her own early fear of the Earl, and then to remembering the answer she had given when he challenged her on that. "I'm scared *for* you now." The fey feeling grew stronger. Questions that seemed to be connected with it began to surface in her mind; the questions that Archie Meikle had once refused to answer. She let the first of them float free on the loose, drifting tide of their conversation.

"Does Lord Garvald know about the Ballinford doom?"

The Earl was sitting with his head leaning back against the tree trunk. Her question brought a sudden stillness to his bulky form. Then, quietly, he answered,

"There was no way I could shield him against knowledge that's common property."

Silence then; everything so silent that she could hear her own breathing. And still no movement from him; no movement anywhere now, not even the white falling of the snow. Another question had surfaced, and when she allowed that one also to drift out from her, she was aware of her voice sounding eerily loud in the stillness.

"How did your brother die—the older brother who had to die before you could be the Earl?"

He sat for so long without speaking that she thought he wasn't going to answer at all. But finally he did, in a voice that had no expression of any kind in it.

"I shot him."

She was still trying to grapple with the enormity of this answer, when the Earl began giving her back question for question.

235

"How much do you know about the Ballinford doom, Jinty?"

"Just what Archie Meikle told me, years ago."

"And what did Archie tell you?"

She could remember exactly what Archie had said; and obediently, word for word, she recited it to him. *"There's never yet been an eldest son of that family has lived to succeed his father. Wars, diseases, accidents—there's been a variety of causes for that. But whatever the cause, the result is always the same. The eldest son dies. A younger son succeeds to the title, lands, money—everything. That's been the way of it for hundreds of years now. That's the doom on the Ballinfords."*

"Wars, diseases, accidents . . ." In a murmur, when she had finished, the Earl repeated the words. His voice trailed into nothing. Then he began to speak again, rapidly this time, and with a rising note of anguish in his voice.

"His name was Hugh. My brother's name was Hugh. He was a year older than I. He was everything that I wasn't—clever, good-natured, open and bright as the sun. A beautiful boy—beautiful! I loved him. I was given a gun for my fourteenth birthday, a double-barrelled twelve-bore. We had a quarrel over it—my fault. I was selfish. Didn't want Hugh to handle *my* present. And I'd disobeyed the rules about always un-loading as soon as the shoot was finished. I grabbed it from him. He held on. The gun went off—in his face. Bright face all shattered, all messed up. And he took so long to die—weeks, weeks! I prayed for him to die, to be out of pain, to be rid of his shattered face. . . ."

She sat appalled at the dreadful flood of memory her questions had unlocked, yet still his voice went on, "But I had to go on living with the memory of it, and with the guilt of Hugh's death. I've never handled a gun since, except when I had to in the Great War; and afterwards, with the Whites in Russia. And always then, with the hope of getting myself killed. Always then, too, with the knowledge that I might be killing someone as bright and beautiful as Hugh. That's been another part of the guilt—because it's always the best ones who die, you know. But none of it was ever any use—not the fighting, not one of all the dangers I courted after the fighting failed me. None of those could kill me either. And not any of the wild living, the drinking, the parties I gave, could ever, ever make me forget the guilt."

She didn't say anything when that long cry of anguish came to an end at last, but there was a pity sharp as pain burning through the numbness of cold in her. He spoke again, after a while; questioning.

"And why? What's it all been for? They tell old wives' tales about the Ballinford doom, of course, but nobody really knows how or why it started. It's as if—as if God had just opened his mouth one day and spat carelessly in *our* direction. A meaningless sort of curse; that's what it is. And there's no way at all of breaking it, unless—"

The head leaning against the tree trunk turned. The

shadowy shape of his face inclined towards her.

"Can *you* see what that way is?"

She had thought about this so often since Archie had told her about the doom, that the answer came pat to her lips. "Yes, of course. If the father died before the son, the son would be bound to inherit."

"That's it," he agreed. "That's exactly it. But it would still be only a beginning, you know. It wouldn't affect just one generation. The pattern to the doom is an ancient one, after all; and who knows how many Ballinfords now past have died just because they *expected* an accident to happen to them? Sort of willed it on themselves, you might say, without realizing that's what they were doing. But if once that pattern was changed, d'you see, there'd be a change too, in these expectations. There'd be nothing like the same belief in the doom, in fact; and that could be the very thing to break it, finally, for all the future generations of Ballinfords. D'you follow me?"

"Yes." She nodded. "You're right there, I suppose."

"Then think of this." His voice took on a harsher note. "Garvald's bound to have seen the answer to the whole thing as clearly as you or I; but he knows dam' well, too, that I'm strong enough to last for another twenty years. Yet he's a good lad, and he loves me. And so where does that leave him? With his feelings for me slowly poisoned—that's where. And there you have the real bitterness that every generation of our family has had to suffer. There's the real evil that would finally be broken with the breaking of the Ballinford doom. D'you

238

follow me there too, Jinty?"

"Yes," she said again; and this time was aware of her answer as no more than a shocked whisper floating down into the black void his words had opened for her. A face looked up from its depths—Garvald's face wearing the look of torment she had glimpsed as he was carried off in the Rolls on the harvest Sunday when the Earl and Mr. Elphinston had roared at one another over the Ballinford doom. She closed her eyes against the sight of it, but could not close her mind against its new understanding of that look; nor could she escape the realization that there must have been other occasions when the same torment had shown through the surface quiet of Lord Garvald's face. Uneasily, as she wondered how many these occasions had been, she waited for the Earl to speak again.

He was leaning forward, elbows on knees, face pressed against his upraised palms. After a moment or two like this he drew his hands slowly away, looked sideways at her, and said,

"It's odd you should be here tonight."

"*You of all people.*" That was what his tone implied; but when she didn't remark on this, he went on,

"We were talking about courage, remember? Your mother has the enduring kind. Meg has the courage to live. But there's still another form of courage—the opposite one to Meg's. And yet—it's such a lonely one. And courage needs—should have, some sort of witness to it."

"*You'll know when it's going to happen.*" Now she

239

knew what he had meant, that night in the library! Now she understood the reason for the fey feeling. It surged to the surface of her mind, and came out in words.

"There'll be me," she told him. "I'll know."

He nodded, staring at her, then said slowly, "That's right. There will be you. I wonder—? Is that why I've sat here talking to you?"

"You were drunk," she said, "or you wouldn't have bothered."

"I'm not really drunk now." He rose as he spoke, and stood staring into the woods. "And so what am I doing, talking to you like this, letting you say such things to me? I was drunk enough at the party, God knows, and Archie was the last person I spoke to before I left it. Yet still I didn't give him the least hint of what's in my mind—and I've never had a better friend than Archie Meikle."

"But I don't need hints," she pointed out. "You told me yourself I'd know when it was going to happen—remember?"

"I remember." He nodded, but in a distracted way, as if there was something else troubling him now. His gaze came back to her, and abruptly he warned, "It's a crime, you know. At least, the church calls it a crime, and the law is benighted enough to agree with that."

"But that's crazy!" The amazement in her voice made him laugh briefly, grimly.

"Crazy or not," he said, "the fact is that it could mean a lot of unpleasantness—not just for my son, but for everybody connected with me. For a start, there's Elphinston. He could refuse a consecrated burial, and think of the newspaper headlines then! Then there's the doom—the reason for it all. It's got to seem to be an accident, something that was just fated to happen; because that's the only way to convince Garvald—and everyone else too—that the doom really has been broken. And that means you mustn't tell anyone. No one. Not ever. D'you understand?" He bent towards her with the question, and added quietly, "Yours must be a silent form of witness, Jinty."

She looked up at him. His face was only inches from hers. She felt so sorry for him then that she wanted to beg him to change his mind, but the cold steadily gripping her had begun to make her head feel fuzzy. She didn't seem able to think properly any more, and it was an effort now to form words.

"It's all right," she managed eventually. "I'm good at keeping my mouth shut."

"Promise?"

"Promise."

A hand came out to touch lightly on her cheek. "You're freezing," he said. "Will you get back to your parents now?"

She mumbled assent. The face above the hand withdrew. She heard him say under his breath, *"Ballinford, if you're not still drunk, you must be crazy!"* Then he was moving away from her, a dark shape among the taller dark shapes of the trees, his footsteps soundless on the new, soft snow. She thought of rising to run after him, but the thought couldn't will her body into action. The moving shape seemed unreal, like something she had dreamed of as she sat there getting colder and colder. Her eyes were smarting with the cold. She closed them, and let all the talk she had had with the Earl slide into the same dreamlike feeling.

A voice started up in her mind; a small, distant voice that warned her she would freeze to death if she continued to sit there. She felt vaguely frightened, but she wanted to sleep, to fall deeply, deeply asleep; and so she compromised with the voice. She would sleep for only a few minutes, and then she would get up and stamp about to get warm, and everything would be all right then. The voice argued plaintively that she was kidding herself, that she couldn't be sure of waking when she should, but she ignored the warning. The voice receded, and died in a vast black silence.

Torchlight startled her awake. The beam was dazzling close. She moaned in protest at its brightness against her smarting eyes; and over her moan, a voice shouted,

"She's here! Morrison, I've found her!"

It was a man's voice. She became aware of other men with torches, converging on the shout. The first man gripped her arm, trying to pull her to her feet, but her body was locked in its crouched position. She gave a cracked scream of pain. He let her go, and said in a shocked voice,

"Good grief, lassie! You're fair paralyzed with the cold!"

The other men were crowding in on her. Her father

was there. She found herself being bundled around with blankets, a cup of something hot put to her lips. She sipped, choked, sipped again, then drank gratefully. It was her father who held the cup. Mr. Elphinston appeared at his shoulder, saying,

"So she's all right, is she?"

"Aye, thank God," her father told him; and Mr. Elphinston said,

"Amen to that, Morrison. It *is* only God's mercy we didn't find her dead, as well as the Earl."

Memory of the Earl came flooding back to her; a wild, confused memory of talking to him only a few minutes before the torch was shone into her face.

"But he was here," she said stupidly. "Just minutes ago. I was talking to him. He can't be dead—"

Just in time she stopped herself from adding "yet." Her father said in a puzzled voice,

"But he couldn't have been here minutes ago, Jinty. It's an hour since they found him dead, with his neck broken, at the foot of Temple Rock."

The man who had found her said, "She's confused about the time, Morrison. She was asleep when I found her."

"But if she talked to him," Mr. Elphinston said, "that could be important. You heard what the police said. From the signs at the top of that crag, there's some doubt over how the Earl came to fall from its edge."

"Here now, wait!" another voice exclaimed; but, brusquely, Mr. Elphinston cut the voice short.

"There's no use procrastinating, Meikle. If she can

243

throw light on the tragedy, we ought to know about it." His face poked forward into the torchlight; thin, sharp, like a ferret's face probing. "Now, Jinty," he began; and then the questions came fast, one after the other.

Had the Earl been drunk, or sober? How long did he talk? What did he say? Why had he talked to her? Where had he come from? Where did he go when he left her?

She tried to answer the way she knew she had to. She tried hard to fend off the probing ferret face. But the more she stuttered in her replies, the more insistently Mr. Elphinston went at her. And other faces joined his, all of them drawing close together within the ring of torchlight, all the mouths in the faces competing to shoot questions at her. She was like a rabbit at one end of a burrow with the ferret peering in at her, and the encircling faces were those of the men who had gathered to egg the ferret on—all, except two of them.

Her father and Archie Meikle were the two who hung back from the questioning; and it was they who saved her at last, with a look flung from one to the other, and then a sudden forward movement that swept her up from the ground to be carried off between them.

"You're fine, you're fine now," her father tried to soothe the outburst of weeping that came from her relief at this. And over his shoulder, as they strode away with her, Archie flung at the rest of them,

"And you lot, think shame of tormenting the bairn like that! If she does have a story, she'll tell it when she's good and ready to talk. And then she'll tell it where she should—to the police!"

18

Archie Meikle came out of the Fiscal's office and walked rapidly away down the corridor.

"Your turn now," Jinty's mother said.

Jinty glanced at her, but didn't risk an answer. Archie hadn't so much as turned his head in the direction of the waiting room, and it had been impossible to guess how his interview with the Fiscal had gone. The woman clerk appeared with her sheet of paper and her vague, meaningless smile.

"Janet Beatrice Morrison," she read from the paper, and then said, "The Fiscal will see you now, Jan—er, Miss Morrison."

Jinty rose to her feet. Her mother made to rise also, looking uncertainly from Jinty to the clerk.

"I have to see him by myself," Jinty said. Her mother opened her mouth as if to protest against this, but closed it again when the clerk said,

"Er—yes, Mrs. Morrison. The interview is private."

She had begun moving off as she spoke. Jinty fo
lowed her. At the door of the Fiscal's office she looke
back towards her mother, and saw her trying to smi
encouragement. She nodded, forcing her own featur
into an answering smile. The clerk swung the do
wider for her. She walked forward, with the door clo
ing again behind her and the Procurator Fiscal lookir
up from his desk at her entrance.

A rush of thoughts went through her mind. M
Talbot was a small man. His desk was huge. He looke
islanded behind it. There was a chair in front of th
desk. Was that where she was supposed to sit? As sh
hesitated, he waved towards the chair and said,

"Well, do be seated, Miss—er—"

"Jinty," she told him.

He took off his reading glasses and smiled at her. H
eyes were blue, and now that she could see them witl
out the barrier of the glasses, they had a shrewdness i
them that dismayed her.

"Ah, yes," he said. "Every Janet I've ever known ha
been called Jinty. Delightful custom, isn't it, ou
Scottish way of finding diminutives for every name?

Small talk. The man was just trying to be pleasan
she realized; and sat down, feeling embarrassed at n
being able to reply in kind. The Fiscal shuffled som
papers on his desk, cleared his throat, and said,

"Well, then—er—Jinty. May I take it that you undei
stand the nature of my official function?"

"Yes, sir," she told him. "My mother explained it t
me."

247

Accident, accident, accident . . .

"And so you know, don't you, that it's my duty now to try to establish the reason for the sudden death of the late Earl of Ballinford?"

"Yes, sir."

"And to decide from these private inquiries whether or not the public interest demands that I pursue my findings in open court? You understand that too, don't you?"

I swear by Almighty God, as I shall answer to Him at the Great Day of Judgment . . . Mr. Talbot was polishing his spectacles, waiting for her to speak.

"Don't be frightened," he encouraged. "You can take your time to answer anything I ask."

"Yes, sir," she managed. "Thank you, sir. I understand."

"Good, good." Mr. Talbot nodded, looking relieved. "We can proceed then." More shuffling of papers, another clearing of his throat, the blue eyes looking keenly at her again—*Yours must be a silent form of witness.* . . .

"There is no question of foul play, of course," Mr. Talbot said. "Police investigations to date have satisfactorily ruled that out as a possibility. Er—I wonder if you can think why, Jinty."

She guessed at the reason, remembering the snow that had started falling just before she left the ice-party.

"Footprints," she said. "There was fresh snow that night, and if there had been anyone else at the top of

Temple Rock, the police would have found his footprints."

The words were no sooner out of her mouth than she realized how she had blundered. She had meant the Fiscal to think she was stupid; but he had just tested her, tried her to see how well she could put two and two together. And she had walked straight into his trap. She bit her lip in annoyance at herself, then tried to look gratified as Mr. Talbot said,

"Good, good. That is exactly why. There were no footprints on Temple Rock that night, apart from those of the Earl, either on the path to the top of the crag or on the summit itself. *But*, it is also the question of footprints that provides one of the puzzling features of the Earl's death—because, you see, his footprints led to the very edge of the precipice from which he fell; and in the final pair of prints, there was a depth of indentation which showed that he stood there for some minutes before his fall. But that still did not tell the police *how* he came to fall."

"He was drunk!" In the effort to keep the nervous fear she felt from showing in her voice, Jinty spoke more vehemently than she had intended. Mr. Talbot's eyebrows rose. He looked thoughtfully at her, and then said,

"Well, now, Jinty, that's an expression of opinion on your part, isn't it? Which is rather different, you'll agree, from making a statement of proven fact. And so, let's just go back a bit, shall we, and work methodically through the chain of events that led you to make that assumption about the Earl; starting, maybe, with what you observed about him at the party—h'mm?"

There was the conversation she'd had with Mr. Ramenski. She detailed that to the Fiscal, harking back to her winter at the Hall to explain the reason for it. Mr. Talbot took notes as she spoke, but had nothing to say until his next question.

"And what time was it when the Earl came on you in the woods?"

Time? Time hadn't existed for her that night. She looked at him in confusion, and then remembered her glimpse of Archie and the Earl talking and laughing together.

"I saw Archie Meikle and the Earl talking just before I left the party," she offered. "Did Mr. Meikle tell you about that talk?"

Mr. Talbot nodded. "He did. It happened between ten-fifteen and ten-thirty."

"Then it couldn't have been long after that when the Earl came on me, because I didn't walk far into the woods, and I was just beginning to get really cold from sitting still when he stopped beside me."

"And when he spoke to you then, what was your impression of him?"

"Well—" She hesitated, cautioning herself against that earlier vehemence. "I was sitting at the foot of a tree, and he had to put a hand on the tree trunk to steady himself when he bent down to me. And he rambled on, the way men do when they're drunk."

"Was his speech slurred?"

"Oh, no!" She was so shocked to think anyone could imagine the Earl losing his dignity to such an extent, that she forgot immediately the caution she had given herself.

"So you could hardly describe him as really drunk, after all," Mr. Talbot remarked. And once again, she was aware of having blundered.

Mr. Talbot put down his pen and looked intently at her. "You see, Jinty," he went on, "there would seem to have been no reason for the Earl to have left the party when he did, unless he was so drunk that he didn't know what he was doing then. But your statement concurs with that of Mr. Meikle in showing that— although the Earl did have a fair amount of drink taken just prior to his death, he was by no means intoxicated. And so, it seems, we must look for a reason, after all. Why did he, at the height of a highly successful celebration, just abandon the whole proceedings to walk off into the woods?"

"Maybe he was like me," she said. "Maybe he just wanted to go off by himself and be quiet for a while. That was my only reason for going into the woods."

"Yes, yes," Mr. Talbot acknowledged. "So I understood from your statement to the police. And it's reasonable, I suppose, to think that the Earl may have felt similarly at the time. But that still doesn't explain why he climbed Temple Rock, and stood in that very dangerous position, so close to its edge."

She saw the escape route his line of argument had

left her, and darted quickly for it. "But the Earl was always doing dangerous things! Really dangerous ones. He was like that."

"Mmm." Mr. Talbot sat considering her answer before he asked, "A man of impulse, attracted to danger—is that your estimate of him?" She nodded. He made another note, and then looked up to say, "Well, that certainly squares with the opinion that seems generally to have been held of him."

Jinty sat back, feeling some of the tension go out of her. The Fiscal hadn't been laying traps for her, after all, she thought. He had just been probing to see if she thought differently from other folk about the Earl. And now that he was sure this wasn't so, he would stop wondering if there had been some mystery about the Earl leaving the party and climbing the crag.

"Now then, Jinty," Mr. Talbot's voice broke into her thoughts. "Let's go further back in time with the next few questions. First of all, how long have you known the Earl?"

"A long time, sir," she told him. "All my life, in fact."

"Did you know him well?" She hesitated, and the Fiscal added, "Perhaps I should rephrase that. Did you have much contact with him?"

"Quite a bit, sir. He was often in the village. And then there was last winter, when I worked at the Hall."

"He was a man of very great wealth and high position, Jinty. Was he snobbish about that?"

"Not in the least, sir." She almost smiled, the idea of the Earl as a snob was so ridiculous. "He spoke to everybody. And Mr. Meikle—Archie Meikle the black-smith, was his best friend."

"So I've gathered," Mr. Talbot said dryly. "But even Mr. Meikle agrees he was a man with many facets to his character. Is that how he appeared to you?"

"Yes, sir. He wasn't easy to understand."

"Did you like him?"

"Not at first, sir. At first, I was scared of him; but after a while—" She hesitated again. "I—well, I came to feel sorry for him."

"That's rather a strange statement, isn't it? Why should you feel sorry for a man of such power and riches?"

"I felt he was a sad man, sir—deep down sad, I mean. And lonely."

"Hmmm. But he was also notorious in certain ways, I gather. There was a nickname for him, in fact—'the bad old Earl.' What did you think of that?"

She felt a sudden dislike of this little man with the dry, lawyerly voice and the composed manner. Her mind supplied a contrasting image of the Earl poised on the cliff edge, falling from there like a strong old tree, storm-destroyed at last. *There's still another form of courage. . . . And yet—it's such a lonely one.* Had he thought of that again, she wondered, before he let himself fall? And out of all this came an impulse to stand up and shout,

"What d'you mean 'bad'? He was a doomed man, and he knew it. All his life he knew it. Is that what you call 'bad,' fighting to forget that?" But the little man

253

wouldn't have understood what she was talking about. Or would he have understood only too well? In sudden fear that any answer at all might tell the Fiscal more than she had intended, she retreated even deeper into silence; and eventually he said,

"Well, perhaps it wasn't entirely proper of me to ask that. One shouldn't expect a girl of your age, after all, to pass moral judgments on her elders. But talking of what is fair and what isn't, Jinty, I think this is the moment that I should explain certain things to you. About the law, that is."

"Yes, sir?" *Look attentive. Don't let him see you're scared.*

"The law, Jinty—" The Fiscal permitted himself a small, thin smile. "The law may sometimes seem to be foolish, but there is always good reason for its apparent vagaries. In the present situation, for instance, we both know that the Earl's death was not due to foul play, and it therefore becomes my duty to question you on possible alternatives to that. But it is also my duty to ask questions in such a way that I do not lay these alternatives before you. Otherwise, I could influence the answers you might give; and so I must try to arrive at the truth through what might seem to be rather an oblique form of questioning. D'you follow me?"

"Yes, sir." Jinty kept her eyes on the Fiscal's face, wondering why he took such a long way around to avoid mentioning the word "suicide." He was like an owl, she thought, with that sharp-featured face and those big, round spectacles; a prim, dangerous little owl. The owl-face nodded at her, and said briskly,

"Good, good. We can get back, then, to that night of the ice-party. From your statement to the police, and from what you've already told me today, it seems you knew the Earl well enough to be on talking terms with him. It's very understandable, therefore, that his chance encounter with you just prior to his death, would lead to some degree of conversation. But it's the content of that conversation which is important to me now—not just because you knew the Earl but because you were the last person to see him alive. Is that clear?"

"Yes, sir." This was the big, the real danger looming up now, and she could only whisper her answer.

"Very well, then. We've established that the Earl was to a certain extent under the influence of alcohol; and men in that condition tend to speak with unaccustomed frankness. That will make what you have to say to me all the more important. Therefore"—Mr. Talbot rose from his desk and walked towards the window on the left-hand side of it—"take your time, Jinty. Think as you speak; and tell me as much as you can remember of what was said between the two of you that night."

Mr. Talbot was standing with his back to the window now. Jinty looked towards him, trying to read the expression on his face, but the light behind him had put this into deep shadow. Talking to him was like talking to a man in a mask, she thought, and made a halfhearted attempt to play for time.

"Well, sir, he talked an awful lot—because of being drunk, you see. It was a rambling sort of conversation,

255

too; and me being a bit dopey with the cold, I didn't even hear some of what he said."

"I understand that, Jinty. But I still want to hear all you can remember of it."

"There was the party to begin with." Deliberately switching her gaze from the threat that the faceless face seemed to pose, Jinty looked down at the toes of her shoes and began talking. "We spoke about that, and the Earl said he'd given Lord Garvald a good send-off for his majority. Then he went on about Lord Garvald being able to do anything he liked now that he was twenty-one, and not being his—the Earl's—responsibility any more. He rambled a lot about this, and I wished he'd go away. I stopped listening to him then, but after a while I found he'd sat down on the tree root beside me, and by that time he was talking about the village—the folk in it, and all that, you know. That sort of led on to my own family, and for a good while we talked about them. I got colder and colder sitting there. My head got fuzzy with the cold, and then he got up and said I should get back to my parents. After that, he just walked away. I meant to get up then, but I fell asleep; and that was how they found me."

There was a brief silence, then the Fiscal sighed and said, "That's not a very good report of a conversation, is it?"

Look at him again. He'll think you've got something to hide, if you don't. She looked at the dark blur of face and apologized, "I'm sorry, sir."

The Fiscal gave another sigh. "All right, we'll take it step by step. You must have observed something of the Earl's state of mind in the course of this conversation. How did that strike you?"

"He was—" She searched for the right word. The Fiscal supplied, "Uninhibited?" and she nodded. "That's right. Like he was just saying things as they came into his mind."

"And his manner?"

"Oh—casual, I suppose you could call it."

"Did that manner vary at all?"

"Yes, sir—once."

"When was that?"

"When he talked about a brother of his who had died."

"Why did he talk of that?"

"I asked him. I knew he'd had a brother, and I was curious about the brother dying."

"Wasn't that an odd thing to ask?"

"I didn't think so then, sir. I was talking the same way as he was—just thinking aloud, as it were."

"And how did his manner change when you asked about this brother?"

"He became—upset, sir. Distressed.

"Very distressed?"

"Yes, sir."

"Why?"

"It was the way the brother died that upset him."

"How did that happen?"

257

"The Earl said, 'I shot him.' Then he went on to talk about it having been an accident when he and his brother were boys."

"Did this distress of his continue?"

"No, sir. He went sort of thoughtful after that."

"And what did he talk about when he 'went thoughtful'?"

"About the Ballinford doom."

"What did he say about that?"

"He said it was a meaningless sort of curse. He said it was just like God had turned one day and spat at his family."

"Jinty—" The Fiscal moved slowly back to his desk, sat down, and turned his intent look on her. "Jinty, what do you know about the Ballinford doom?"

"Just what I've heard people say, sir; that the eldest son always dies before he can inherit. Oh—and that it's gone on for a long time. Hundreds of years, they say."

"Correct, yes. And can you think of any way that doom could be broken?"

The Fiscal had leaned his elbows on the desk, with his hands making a steeple-shape in front of his face. She could see only his eyes above the tip of the steeple, and they seemed keener than ever. She met their gaze, deliberately letting puzzlement creep into her own.

"Broken, sir? What—? I'm not sure what you mean."

"I mean that there is one way the doom could be avoided in any given generation. One way only. Can you see what that way is?"

The head leaning against the tree trunk, the shadowy face inclined towards her . . .

She kept her own face blank, let her mouth fall open a little. Then she frowned, with fingers pulling at the corner of her mouth in the gesture that came naturally to her when she was baffled by a problem in mathematics. The Fiscal allowed the concealing hands to drop away from his face, and said impatiently,

"All right, all right. If you can't see it, you can't. Now then—"

He broke off there, as he realized the flush of relief springing up in her face and took this to be one of embarrassment.

"Oh, come now!" With kindliness replacing the irritation in his voice, he told her, "There's no need to be ashamed of not seeing the answer. I've asked the same question of others older than you, you know. And none of them saw it." He smiled at her, and with her flush beginning to fade then, she attempted an answering smile. "That's better," he encouraged. "We can't all think like lawyers, can we?"

"No, sir." Dutifully she broadened her smile in reply to the little pleasantry, but let her gaze go back to her feet as she did so, in case he might read in it her real feelings. The rustling of papers from his desk made her look up again.

"Now then, Jinty." Mr. Talbot was leaning forward over the papers, his smile gone, his eyes raking her as shrewdly as before. "I was about to ask you some final questions, and I want you to think very carefully before you answer them. Will you?"

She nodded. He held her gaze a moment longer, then abruptly he asked,

"When the Earl left you that night, did he say where he was going?"

"No, sir."

"In all your conversation with him, was there any point at all when he mentioned that?"

"No, sir."

"Did he even hint what his destination might be?"

"No, sir."

"Did he announce any intention of any kind?"

"No, sir."

"Or even hint at an intention?"

"No, sir." She had known without any need of hints. And that was how it had been when they spoke about it—each of them understanding the other without ever having to say so. That meant she was still on the right side of the law with her answers. And she was still managing to live up to the last *"Promise."* Yet there was some trap hidden in this new line of questioning. She sensed it; but when, how, would it be sprung?

Mr. Talbot looked up from the notes he had been making. "I want you to think about the summit of Temple Rock," he told her; "about the ruins of the castle and the small chapel which were built by some far-off ancestors of the late Earl of Ballinford. Crusading knights, I believe they were. Are you aware of that fact?"

Daydreaming in class about the stone knights . . .
Miss Carson's history lesson . . .

"Yes, sir, I learned about it at school."

"Then let me take you back briefly to the matter of the footprints. Police investigation has shown that these led first into that ruined chapel; and it was from there that the Earl proceeded to the point from which he fell. Also, as it was with the footprints at the edge of the cliff, the depth of indentation in the final pair of prints in the chapel shows that the Earl stood there for some minutes before walking to his death."

The Fiscal was looking hard at her, and she couldn't conceal her surprise at this new piece of information. "Now," he finished, "do you have any idea of why he should have done that?"

She couldn't answer at first. She was too caught up in the sudden realization that the Earl could have had only one purpose in going into the chapel. The stone knights, his ancestors, had also prayed there; and where else would he want to be when he made his own last prayer? Something in her was deeply shaken by the thought of the loneliness he must have felt standing there; yet the something also recognized itself as being the very feeling that was leading her into the trap she had sensed. And the Fiscal was pressing now for her answer, his voice sharpening as he asked,

"Well, Jinty? Supposing the Earl did fall from the cliff as a result of some impulse of drunken bravado. Does it not seem curious that he should take time to visit the chapel before carrying out that impulse?"

The trap was about to close on her. "He was—" Her lips had gone dry with fear, and words were difficult to shape. "He was proud of being the Earl," she managed at last; and immediately Mr. Talbot shot back at her,

"You said earlier that he wasn't a snob."

She had simply been playing for time with her answer; but now, it seemed, that had just got her even deeper into the mire. She hunted in her mind for safe ground, but could only say defensively,

"I didn't mean proud in that way. I just meant proud of belonging to an ancient family. And having men like the Crusading knights for his ancestors was part of that."

"Hmm. So you feel this is all of a piece with the Earl's final action—is that it? First of all he reflects on the ancestors who performed deeds of derring-do; and from this, is foolishly inspired to court danger on his own behalf. Is that what you're implying?"

The Fiscal had made the case for her, she realized; and made it much better than she herself could have done. She nodded, relief surging through her.

"Yes, sir. You could put it that way, I suppose."

"I see." Mr Talbot spent further moments writing, then looked up again to say, "One final question, then, Jinty. I understand from Mr. Meikle that the Earl had a certain fondness for you. And you were the last person he spoke to before his death. What kind of leave did he take of you? Can you give me the exact words of it— the very last words he spoke on this earth?"

But it hadn't been to her that the Earl had spoken his last words on earth. It had been to himself he'd said, *"Ballinford, if you're not still drunk, you must be crazy!"* The Fiscal was waiting, pen poised above the list of his notes. She spoke slowly, carefully.

"I was so cold, I think he was worried about me. He touched me on the cheek and said, 'You're freezing.' Then he asked me, 'Will you get back to your parents now?' I told him I would, and that was the very last thing he said to me before he went away."

"Thank you, Jinty." The Fiscal made a last note, laid down his pen, lined up the papers on his desk, and said, "Well, that seems to decide the matter. And, you see, you did manage to remember quite a lot of that conversation, after all."

She looked at the notes lying neatly aligned beside the pen, and nerved herself to ask,

"What *have* you decided, sir?"

The Fiscal had been looking satisfied. Now, suddenly, he was severe again, staring disapprovingly as he told her,

"You're not supposed to ask me that."

"I'm sorry, sir, but—"

"But what?"

She was a minor, she reminded herself. He wouldn't think the excuse she had in mind was an odd one. "It's the idea of Court, sir," she told him. "I mean, if there's to be a Public Inquiry. I've never been in any kind of Court before, and I'd be nervous of that."

"Oh. I see. Well, yes, I suppose that could be rather

frightening for a youngster." With neat, precise movements, the Fiscal took off his glasses and began polishing them on the hem of his lawyer's robe. "And with that in mind," he went on, "I think that I could make an exception to the rule in your case."

The glasses were polished to his satisfaction. He put them on again, stood up, and said,

"On the balance of evidence, Jinty, I have decided that the Earl's death was simply a tragic accident. There will be no further inquiry into it. And so—er—thank you for attending here, and—er—"

She was being dismissed! It was all over, and the little man was trying to get rid of her! The word "accident" rang so loudly in her ears that it was a moment before she grasped what was happening. She got to her feet, clumsily, blushing and stammering in reply to his polite hope that he hadn't kept her too long. Then, without transition it seemed, she was outside the door of his office, her mother's worried face was looming towards her, and the two of them were walking rapidly away through the echoing corridors of the Sheriff Court Building.

19

It was cold at the bus stop. Jinty huddled into herself and let the echo of *"Promise?" "Promise,"* go singingly through her mind. The words warmed her as much as the heavy velour cloth of her school coat. But her mother was shivering, she noticed; and wished, as she did every winter, that all the money didn't have to be spent on expensive Academy uniform.

"Have we long to wait for the bus?" she asked.

"Not long." Her mother caught the glance that had gone with the question, held it with her own, and asked, "How did you get on with the Fiscal?"

"All right."

"That's no answer, girl!"

The exasperation in her mother's voice startled her. And there was an expression on her mother's face—a look of burning anxiety, which was another thing she hadn't expected.

"What did you tell him?" Her mother was determined

to find out, she realized, but still she resisted.

"Just what I had to."

"Go on. You know it's not enough to say that." She tried to look away, but her mother's urgent voice went on, "Jinty, I want to know what he's decided, and you've got to tell me."

"I can't. Telling me was just a favor on his part. And if there is to be an Inquiry, there'll be a notice in the newspaper, won't there?"

"I know that. But can't you see, girl? That'll mean even more waiting for all of us. And surely to goodness we've been patient enough with you!"

The possible meaning of her mother's words broke on her with a shock of realization that took her breath away. She stammered in trying to voice the questions that sprang immediately to her mind; and, impatiently, her mother interrupted,

"I know. I know. You thought you were the only one who understood. You just didn't take account of the fact that all of us have known the Earl—and all about the doom, too—a lot longer than you have. And we guessed, girl. Of course we guessed—or some of us did, at least. But you were still the only one who might really *know*. And you're so young. How could we depend on you to parry the kind of questions we knew the Fiscal would ask? That's been our problem all along. And that's why I've *got* to have an answer from you now."

"I didn't tell him anything the Earl wouldn't have wanted me to say." Astonishment was still making it difficult to speak, and the words came gaspingly from her. "He's decided it was an accident, Mam. But Mam—"

The tenseness in the face turned to her began to slacken. Held breath came out from it in a sigh of "Thank God!" She pressed on over the sound,

"But Mam, if you'd known how scared I was of all those questions! Why didn't you say you'd guessed? You could have coached me, told *me* what to say!"

Her mother sighed again. "Oh, Jinty, how could we? Telling you what to say would have amounted to interfering with a legal process—and that's a serious business. Not that there weren't some who wanted to try it, mind you—your father and Archie Meikle among them. But I put my foot hard down on that! And then there was the Earl himself. Whatever he did say to you, he said it because he trusted you. You had to earn that trust, lassie. And you had to earn it alone."

"But Archie did try to tell me, after all!" The shock of realization was fading now, and as her mind began working normally again she remembered all the ominous hints Archie had given about the Fiscal. "D'you remember, Mam? When he spoke about the way the Fiscal would put all our evidence together to get a whole picture of the Earl, and I asked what I should say about the Ballinford doom?"

"Aye, Archie." Her mother's voice had a note of dry amusement in it now. "He kept trying till the end, that one. But I still managed to shut him up about it!"

She said reproachfully, "But you tried yourself, Mam. There was one time there, in the waiting room, when you were all ready to tell me what to say. And you wanted to come into the Fiscal's office with me."

"I know that." Her mother flushed a little with the admission. "It was just seeing you so young, and on your own. It weakened me."

The bus drew alongside. They got in, and sat for a while without talking. It was maybe the sudden lifting of the strain, Jinty told herself, but now she felt too tired to think, let alone talk; but as the bus passed the Academy, her attention woke again to the sight of all the activity around its gates. She glimpsed Mr. Verity shuffling his way through a mob of pupils returning after dinner break, hair as wild as usual, long scarf trailing as raggedly as ever behind him, and pointed him out to her mother.

"That crazy-looking character there," she remarked. "D'you see him? That's old Verity, the Art master."

Interested, her mother peered towards the shuffling figure. "The same one who gives you such good marks?"

"Yes. But Mam—" She hesitated, and then said with a rush, "He might look daft, and people say he is, but I don't think so. Not really. Because he knows I can't draw. And he's told me that. That's why I'll never be an artist, Mam. Not any kind of an artist, however much you might want it that way."

"All right, Jinty." Her mother drew back from the window, a tight, defensive look on her face. "You weren't the only one in that waiting room with a lot of time to think things out. And you don't have to spell your case out for me now, the way Linda did with hers."

They settled into silence again. But that had been the first time since the night of the great burst-up that her mother had voluntarily mentioned Linda's name; and after a while, Jinty couldn't help herself asking,

"Do you miss Linda, Mam?"

"That's a pale word for the feeling I have. She's my child. Nothing can alter that. But—" Her mother's straight back grew even straighter. Without looking around, she asked, "Can you really see Linda ever being one of the family again? Even if she wanted to— which she doesn't. And so there's nothing else I can do, is there, except to put up with the way I feel?"

"Mam—"

"Mphm?"

"What we talked about in the woods—the Earl and myself—was courage. He said you had the courage of endurance."

Her mother said nothing for a few moments. Then, quietly, she asked, "And was he right, d'you think?"

"Yes, Mam."

Now her mother's head did turn, and light caught a glisten of tears from it; but even so, there was something like a smile on the face that said,

"I wouldn't be ashamed to have that for my epitaph, Jinty."

They didn't speak again for the rest of the journey. The return bus from the village to Haimston passed their own at the usual point, and the swish of wheels that had begun whispering *Meg, Meg, Meg . . .* sounded louder and louder on Jinty's inner ear. But they had been gone such a long time! And even if Meg had found the door key in its usual place, would she have lingered so long in the empty house? The bus drew up at the top of the village street, bare fields on one side of it, and on the other, the small white cottages crouching low behind the strips of garden full of snowdrops. Toby . . .

"*Go away,*" she told the small clown-ghost hovering in her mind; but speaking gently, because it was only a small ghost, after all. "*I've got my own life to live, Toby.*"

Her father was standing at the bus stop. He looked pinched with cold, as if he had been waiting there for a long time, meeting one bus after another. His face was anxious, too, and as soon as he had helped her mother off the bus, he said,

"Meg's in the village, Jean. With her baby. But she's not at home. She's—" He stopped short, looking across the street towards a car standing outside Archie Meikle's house. It was Dave Ferguson's car, a Bullnose Morris he had spent weeks working on, in the shed behind the smithy. "She's with Dave now. He came to take her back to their own place. But Jean—Please! Jean!"

Her mother had started across the street, no longer listening to him; and he was following, pleading as he went, with herself trailing disconsolately behind the two of them. "Give them a chance, will you? The girl came in good faith, after all; and neither of them wants another row with you."

Her mother turned to him, with a hand raised to

knock at Archie Meikle's door. But they had been observed from within the house. The door opened without any need for a knock, and Tom Meikle was standing there, question and alarm on his face.

"Tom." Her mother looked him up and down. "I'd have preferred my first sight of my grandchild to be in my own house. But since Meg and the bairn are here with you—"

"Dave's here too," Tom interrupted; but her expression didn't change as she said,

"So I'm told. And as I've always understood it, at least, a child's entitled to both its parents."

The big Viking face looking down at her cleared slowly into a broad smile. "The kettle's on, Mrs. Morrison," Tom said. "You came just at the right time."

An inner door of the house opened as he spoke. Mrs. Tom Meikle's face looked out from the room behind the door, brown-button eyes glancing curiously; and from within the same room came the loud, laughing sound of Meg's voice. Tom turned to lead the way into the house, at the same time throwing back over his shoulder,

"My Dad's in the smithy, Jinty. Will you shout him in for a cup of tea?"

She ran to obey, a sudden shyness making her glad of not having to see Meg and her mother meeting again at last. And of course, she would have to warn Archie what to expect when he went indoors! She found him in the smithy, the jacket of his go-to-meeting flung down over the anvil while he pottered around tidying up the place;

271

and stopped in the doorway, with the old habit of watching him taking its grip on her again.

"Aye, Jinty." He turned to her. "You've got back."

"We've all got back," she told him. "There's tea ready for you. But Mr. Meikle, my Mam's in your house. She's seeing Meg and Dave and the baby. She *wants* to see them!"

Archie grinned. "Then I take it," he said, "that she'll not be averse to seeing me either—not if she's accepted Meg again, at last—eh?"

She grinned back at him, feeling this was answer enough, then saw his face grow sober again as he went on, "But what's caused such a big change in her? That's what I wonder."

"Meg always said she'd never be able to resist the thought of seeing the baby," she told him. "And today, in the waiting room, she was thinking a lot. It was maybe then that she decided."

Archie nodded. "Aye, well, she was sore hurt, of course, your mother; and so it was bound to take time for her to get over it. But I'm glad it's happened this way at last."

Jacket in hand he moved to the doorway, and they walked together to the front door of his house. Archie stopped there, cocking his head to the muted sounds coming from inside, and she read the thought behind the gesture. Once among all the others there, they would have no chance to talk privately, and there were still private things they had to say to one another. Archie turned to her.

"Well, lass? How did it go?"

"Accident," she told him. "The Fiscal put it down as accident."

Archie stared at her for a long moment without speaking. Then, slowly a broad grin spread over his dark, gnomelike features.

"Good for you," he said through the grin. "And good for the Earl, eh? The old devil! So he pulled it off, after all, did he? And got away with it, too! Now that was a *man*, Jinty. Damned if that wasn't a man!"

"When did you guess?" she asked. "He told me that he never even hinted about it to you, when you and he were talking that night."

"Neither he did." Archie's grin had vanished at her question. He was speaking soberly now, even grimly. "But I've dreaded it for years past—ever since that day you told me of his quarrel with old Hell-fire, in fact. And in spite of the way he laughed and joked with me at the party, I saw the way his eyes kept going to young Garvald."

Garvald! Why hadn't she thought of him?

"But Mr. Meikle—!" Mouth open in dismay, she stared at Archie. "If you guessed, and my Mam and Dad and other folks as well, why shouldn't Lord Garvald have guessed, too? And if he has, it won't be any good after all, will it? Garvald will still go on believing in the doom."

Archie shook his head. "Not a bit of it! For a start, there's nobody dared breathe a word to him about any possibility except accident. *I* made sure of that. What's

273

more, I've had a good few talks with him since his father died. He *wants* to believe the doom's broken, and you can take it from me that he does. It's turned out exactly as the Earl wanted, Jinty. Believe me."

"I always have, Mr. Meikle." She said this solemnly, not realizing how over-earnest she sounded until Archie laughed at her for it. She was amused herself, then; but even in the midst of smiling, the impulse came on her to exclaim,

"I'll miss him!"

"Aye, you and me both," Archie agreed. "But I'll tell you something, Jinty. Wherever he is now, he'll miss us—all of us."

That was quite likely too, she thought; and told Archie so. He nodded, pushing open the door of the house. A soft babble of sound reached them then, men's voices, women's voices, baby cries, teacups rattling; and they should have gone towards it. But something kept them both standing there; some sense of the Earl's presence still brooding over the village, it seemed to Jinty. And when Archie spoke again, she realized that he felt the same way.

"He'll not let us alone, will he?" Archie asked quietly. "Can you feel that?"

She nodded. Then, with her gaze travelling up the winding village street towards the farm, and resting finally on the dark edge of Ballinford Woods, she said,

"We're studying a play at school—Shakespeare—and there's a line from it that fits. '*He doth bestride the nar-*

row world like a Colossus.'"

"That's it," Archie exclaimed. "Larger than life—that's what he was. And that's what he always will be."

They looked at one another. "You're maybe not as clever as your sisters," Archie told her, "but you can see things, Jinty. And when you do, you see them whole and clear."

The small domestic babble from indoors grew louder, drawing them at last into the house. She followed Archie towards the sound, wondering if seeing things clear was a gift or a curse. The way things had been for her with the Earl, she thought, she wasn't sure about that. Archie opened the inner door onto a sight of her mother with Meg's baby in her lap; and as he stood aside to let her enter the room, she decided that there wasn't really much point in trying to settle such a question.

She couldn't ever be anybody but herself, after all. And nobody, not even her mother, could make her different from the way she was—the one who always seemed to be standing aside, listening, watching, making connections. *"Seeing with the third eye,"* she thought, suddenly remembering Mr. Verity. Let it go at that, she told herself, and maybe daft old Verity would be proved right after all. All the rest would work itself out eventually the way it was supposed to be for her.

She smiled back at the smiling faces all turned to herself and Archie, all grouped together like some family photograph, and all quite naturally seeming to center

275

around her mother and the baby. Then she went towards them, enjoying the feeling of welcome they gave, yet quietly observing still, their own pleasure in the giving.

Format by Kohar Alexanian
Set in 11 pt. Caledonia
Composed, printed and bound by Vail-Ballou Press, Inc.
HARPER & ROW, PUBLISHERS, INCORPORATED